# FORBIDDEN RANGE

# FORBIDDEN RANGE

Stuart Brock

Chivers Press • Thorndike Press
Bath, England Waterville, Maine USA

This Large Print edition is published by Chivers Press, England, and by Thorndike Press, USA.

Published in 2002 in the U.K. by arrangement with the author c/o Golden West Literary Agency.

Published in 2002 in the U.S. by arrangement with Golden West Literary Agency.

U.K. Hardcover  ISBN 0–7540–4847–0  (Chivers Large Print)
U.K. Softcover   ISBN 0–7540–4848–9  (Camden Large Print)
U.S. Softcover   ISBN 0–7862–3940–9  (Nightingale Series Edition)

The text of this Large Print edition is unabridged.
Other aspects of the book may vary from the original edition.

Set in 16 pt. New Times Roman.

Printed in Great Britain on acid-free paper.

---

**British Library Cataloguing in Publication Data available**

---

**Library of Congress Cataloging-in-Publication Data**

Brock, Stuart, 1917–
      Forbidden range / Stuart Brock.
         p. cm.
      ISBN 0–7862–3940–9 (lg. print : sc : alk. paper)
      1. Large type books.  I. Title.
      PS3539.R565 F67 2002
      813'.54—dc21                  2001058477

# CHAPTER ONE

When Ross Millard pushed his way into the crowded Big Hat Saloon, Rube Overman set himself for trouble. Half-owner of the Big Hat, Overman was a man accustomed to trouble and skilled at stopping it before it could get well started. He watched Ross thrust his way through the crowd, using his heavy shoulders as a battering ram, watched the way the man's steady gray eyes went quickly from one face to another and he lifted one hand in a brief signal.

Eden Bruce, standing at the faro table nearby, saw the gesture and heard Overman call her name, his voice soft, yet urgent. She gave a professional smile to the men around the table and moved toward where Overman's big bulk was squeezed between a small table and the saloon wall. She was a tall girl, lithe and graceful, with a dignity that was almost incongruous against the background of her ornate white satin gown and the noisy surroundings. She stopped by Overman's table and pushed from her face a stray strand of hair so black that it looked almost like jet.

'Ross Millard just came in,' he said.

'I see him.'

The fat around Overman's jowls wrinkled in a scowl. 'I thought he was pushing a herd of horses to the Columbia.' He shifted nearly three hundred pounds of bulk, making the chair groan in protest. 'Whatever it is, he's got that look on his face that means fight.'

The sculptured beauty of Eden's profile was toward Overman as she looked again at Ross Millard. For a moment he saw the professional control slip from her expression and noted the softness there. Then it was gone, covered hurriedly.

'Try dancing with him, honey,' he murmured. 'Draw some of the fire out of him.'

'I wish I could,' she answered. She walked away, moving through the motley crowd of ranchers and miners and loggers that the warm spring night had brought into town and the Big Hat.

Overman put a thick cigar between his lips. It was hard on a girl like Eden, he thought, to feel as she did about a man like Ross Millard. She was bucking a lot—Helene Colson, whose father had left her owner of the Mercantile and the Keeler Hotel, making her the richest woman in this section of Washington Territory, and that vague something called respectability that Ross, for all his unsettled ways, was automatically a part of as son of the sheriff. If, Overman thought, he were twenty years younger and a hundred pounds lighter, he might try to cut Ross Millard out.

He sighed again. Eden had reached Ross and put a hand on his arm to attract his attention. And again her fleeting change of expression gave her away, to the interest of a few sharp observers along the crowded edge of the dance floor. Eden had been an object of interest in the town since she had come from Portland a year before to buy a half interest in the Big Hat. And she had become something of an enigma. Without any hardness, with all the gentle manners of the finishing school she had left at eighteen, she had a way of not only attracting men and holding them, but making them behave. Only a small element in the town did not yet think her respectable. That element was the one Ross Millard had grown up with.

Halfway along the bar, Ross Millard stopped and looked down into the dark eyes of the girl. 'Dance?' he repeated to her question. He was a tall man, wide through the shoulders. His face was lean and craggy and now anger had drawn it even finer so that the bone structure showed through the tautness of his tanned skin.

'Sorry, Eden, but I'm looking for someone.'

'Maybe I can help you find him,' she said. Her voice was rich and deep, poised. 'I usually know who's in here.'

He could still feel the pressure of her fingers on his arm. At almost any other time he would have accepted the invitation to dance and given himself over to the enjoyment of the heady pleasure that Eden's nearness always brought him, but tonight the anger working in him blotted out even the consideration of the girl at his side.

He said, almost roughly, 'Has Monk Ryker come in?'

She should have known, she thought. 'He and Cap Mills are back in the corner,' she said. 'The old man looks to be on another gambling spree and Monk is nursemaiding him.'

'He won't be for long,' Ross said flatly.

'There'll be no fighting in here, Ross.' The very emptiness of her tone brought his head around.

'He sent me off with a bum horse,' he blurted out. 'If I hadn't had to run after a stray, I'd have been across the river before I found out.'

Eden made an almost imperceptible signal behind her back to Rube, a signal that meant she was not having any success. Then she said, 'What would be the point in Monk doing a thing like that? You both work for Cap.'

Ross moved his big shoulders in a shrug. 'How do I know what goes on in Monk's mind—except that he's hated me ever since we were kids. This was supposed to be his trip, but he worked it around until it fell to me. Then he palmed off a lame horse on me.' He started forward, but her hand clamped down, holding him.

'I said there'd be no fighting, Ross. Come on and dance and cool down. Monk won't run

4

away.' She knew it was wasted effort; there were a lot of things about Ross Millard that she admired, but his temper was not one of those things. She had seen it in operation before, and each time she wondered when he was going to learn to control his impulsiveness and put that energy to some practical use.

'This can't wait, Eden. Save that dance for me.'

Reluctantly, she turned away and worked through the crowd on the dance floor to where the piano player was hard at work banging out a tune.

'Mitch,' she said, 'play one long and loud.'

He nodded without lifting his eyes. 'Rube sent Potsy for the sheriff.' His long, sallow face twisted into a smile. 'I'll pound it good and loud, Eden. Maybe you can get enough people out on the floor to keep the fight private.'

She said with quiet bitterness, 'Nothing that Ross Millard gets involved in in this town is ever private, Mitch.'

\*　　　\*　　　\*

Ross found Cap Mills and Monk Ryker at a table along the far wall. They were playing a game of cribbage, and neither man looked as it he were enjoying this way of spending a Saturday night. Cap lifted his thin, seamed face and saw Ross standing behind Monk's chair.

Cap had been pegging and his 'fifteen-two, fifteen-four . . .' trailed off as his pale-blue eyes widened in surprise. 'I thought you'd be camped near the Columbia by this time, boy.'

'So did I,' Ross agreed. 'Ask Monk why I'm not.'

Monk Ryker's heavy torso lifted out of its slouch and he looked around with his dark face blank. 'Why me?' He was a big man, shorter than Ross but thicker in bulk. He had a deep, rumbling voice. He was making an effort to sound injured and only managed to sound ludicrous.

Cap Mills' eyes twinkled as he realized a fight was coming up. He rubbed his hands together. 'Well, since you're back, come and set in and let's have a game. I got a taste for gambling tonight.'

Ross did not even bother to answer. He had his anger focused on Monk Ryker.

He said, 'You gave me a bum horse. It went lame sooner than you figured, or I'd have had to swim back.'

'You're crazy,' Monk retorted. 'I saddled you a good gelding. If you don't know how to ride, it ain't my fault.'

Cap Mills said with soft urging, 'Ross is the best man with a horse in these parts, and you know it.'

Monk shrugged.

Ross said, 'You're going out for that horse and you're going out tonight. And you can

6

push the rest of that herd down to the loading pens.'

'Go sleep it off,' Monk answered. He turned away. 'Finish pegging, Cap?'

Ross reached out and plucked Monk's flat-crowned hat from his head. He tossed the hat on the table and dropped a heavy hand on Monk's shoulder.

'I said tonight.'

He ended the words with a twist, sending Monk and his chair slewing sideways to bank against the wall.

Monk got slowly to his feet. He was half a head below Ross in height but he made up for it in bulk and in the long reach that had given him his nickname. He planted himself squarely on his broad feet.

'You want the sheriff should spank you again for fighting? Go away. I'll ride out with you tomorrow.'

A voice cried, 'Fight!' The piano suddenly lifted to a crescendo of sound and held it, banging lustily. A sad-voiced vocalist tried to make one of his tearful songs loud enough to attract attention.

Ross stepped forward and drove his fist against Monk Ryker's mouth.

Monk spat. He reached out and pushed at Ross's chest, sending him off balance. Ross moved in again, swinging. Monk rolled, taking the blow on his shoulder. Ross kept moving, slashing for Monk's face. Monk looped an easy fist, catching Ross on his jaw and driving him backwards into the circle of watchers that had formed.

Someone pushed and Ross charged, head down. Monk waited for him, his arm cocked and ready. Ross threw a swinging left against Monk's ear. The blow caught Monk off balance and Ross was after him, slashing, battering his face, forcing him up against the long, mahogany bar.

Monk hooked the bar with his elbows and lashed out with both feet. Ross took the bootheels against his chest, and went backward, his arms flailing. He crashed against a thick post which supported the roof. Monk came at him, fists punching, driving forward with the swing of his shoulders behind each blow. Blood spurted from Ross's nose. He tried to block the rain of rock-hard fists that kept him against the post, unable to maneuver.

He could feel himself going. It was just a matter of time now. His wind was gone; his arms felt like weights.

'Break it up!'

Monk stopped and stood with his hands hanging limply, his breath coming from his thick chest in gasps. Ross lifted his head. Dimly he could see his father standing there, the bright star of his office on his cowhide vest, the cold, implacable face above it. As usual, he wore no hat over his kinky iron-gray hair.

'I've said no fighting in this town, You want

8

to fight, take it out of here.' He motioned to both of them.

Ross knew what was coming—a night in jail to cool off. Maybe longer if the sheriff felt like it. He said, 'I started it.'

Cap Mills cackled. 'Take 'em both, Matt. You can't go playing favorites.'

The crowd laughed. Matt Millard flushed. 'No favorites,' he said shortly. 'Come on, Monk.'

'Hey, look, I didn't . . .'

'He said, go,' Cap Mills told Monk. There was force in the old man's voice.

Monk went peacefully. Ross walked ahead, still seeing dimly, his body aching from the blows he had taken. As he stepped into the spring night, someone in the Saturday-night shopping crowd said loudly, 'There goes Ross Millard to jail again. Wonder what he's done now.'

Ross walked on, his head hanging, knowing that his father had heard this, knowing that it meant little to him any more. There were so many things between them that one more— even public ridicule—could have little meaning.

# CHAPTER TWO

Cap Mills watched them go, chuckling. Overman drifted over and took a chair. 'See you got rid of your watchdog, Cap.'

'Sure did. How about a game now?' The old man slapped a hand on the table.

Overman's head wobbled, making his jowls shake. 'You know me better than that, Cap. I don't gamble.'

'You got that new dealer, Walsh, though,' Cap said. 'Maybe he does.'

Overman frowned at the old man. 'Walsh? He hasn't been around long enough for me to know much about him, Cap. Maybe he'll take your shirt.'

'It's mine to lose.'

Overman shook his head again. 'Not in my place it isn't.'

Cap got up, grumbling. 'Getting a game here is harder'n getting a drink at the Ladies' Aid Sunday School.' He stalked off on his long, thin legs and out the door.

Overman watched him go, shaking his head. Eden came up beside him. 'He does love to gamble, doesn't he?'

'Too much. He'd bet his underdrawers in public when he's on a spree like this. Some men get to drinking in spells. Cap gambles.' Overman found his cigar was chewed hopelessly and he threw it at a spittoon. 'If I let him be taken in this place, there isn't a man in town that wouldn't be after my scalp. And he wanted to try the new dealer.'

The girl glanced toward the table where Chet Walsh, the new dealer, was working. He was a slender, handsome man, his hair and thin mustache black, his lean face and quick fingers tanned despite the type of work he did.

She said, 'If I were you, Rube, I'd keep Cap and the other suckers away from him.'

'You've seen something?'

'Nothing definite,' she said quickly. 'It's just a—a feeling.'

Overman didn't question Eden too often when she had her 'feelings.' He had found out from experience—in the year they had been partners—that she was a shrewd business woman. It surprised him every time he realized how much he had come to depend on her. She not only handled the girls and their problems, but she seemed well able to take care of his end of the work as well.

He patted her hand. 'Thanks, Eden.' He rose. 'If you see Cap come back, let me know at once, will you?'

\*     \*     \*

Cap Mills walked for quite a while after he left the Big Hat. The spring night was cool, yet not so cold that it was unpleasant to an old man's

11

bones. He strolled around the town. He enjoyed watching the crowd of farmers and loggers and rangers and their wives doing the Saturday-night buying. Despite what he thought of Helene Colson, he even enjoyed seeing the people flock into her big Mercantile and into the restaurant in her hotel. They were enjoying spending their money the way they wanted to spend it.

Cap Mills had come here before anyone else now here. John Colson had been next and then Rube Overman. With the fine grass in the hill valleys, and the meadows up in the timber, cattle prospered. The flats stretching southward weren't good for much, as dry as they were, but a few farmers worked their distant edges where there were small springs. In time, timber and minerals brought others and the town grew until it was the settlement he saw now.

Cap was proud of having grown up with the town, of having lived his span and more without hurting anyone or anything that he could remember. He had found cattle too time-consuming and had taken to raising horses and that was easier, if less profitable, for a man who no longer wanted to work hard. He had never married. The nearest thing in his mind to a son was Ross Millard, whom he had given work since Ross had been a kid in school. He was fond of Ross and, though he regretted the boy becoming a man and sometimes still acting like a worthless kid, he figured it was Ross's life and it was up to him to handle it as he saw fit.

He walked from the Big Hat at the lower end of Main Street where it straggled out into the desert flats south-eastward toward the railroad, north past the Miners' Supply, then the cross street, past the dark bank, the hardware store, and the freight depot. Crossing the street at its upper end, he went down past the lighted jailhouse, the small restaurant next door, dark now, the big two-story hotel, then the cross street again, below it the Mercantile, the office of the Keeler *Free Press*, two small but busy saloons, and so down to the end of the dusty road where an abandoned smithy sagged against the dark of the night. He started across the street, his old body straight, his thin legs carrying him slowly but easily. The first intimation he had of anyone near was the sharp scuff of a bootsole across wood. He turned, more curious than alarmed. His sharp eyes caught the faint glint of distant light on metal, metal that moved.

He threw himself to one side, his hand clawing for his gun. From behind the abandoned smithy, someone fired and the shot spat dust where Cap Mills had been standing. He fired at the flash as he staggered, off balance. A second shot whispered along the brim of his hat and he snapped an answer at it.

A man cursed in pain. A third shot went

wild, screaming in the air above Cap's head. When he started forward, his gun ready, there was the thud of hoofs on the hard ground. He stopped and slowly holstered his gun. From the saloons a crowd was gathering, coming down toward him. He walked toward them and pushed through, going to the jailhouse.

'What happened, Cap? What was the ruckus?'

'Some bustard tried to snipe me.' The old man kept walking.

To further questions, he said shortly, 'He missed me. Think I pinked him. Made him holler anyway. Now get aside, you. Get aside.'

They let the old man through and he walked with his slow, steady stride up the street to the jailhouse. The sheriff was on his way, hatless as usual, and he pulled up at the sight of the oncoming old man.

'That you, Cap?'

'It was me,' the old man said. He went up the steps and into the lighted office, letting the sheriff follow.

Matt Millard closed the door and then Cap Mills sat down in a chair and looked at his hands. They were shaking. 'I'm getting old, Matt,' he said. 'Like to scared me some.'

'Who was it? What was the idea?'

Cap borrowed a cigar from the sheriff's coat hanging on a nail near him and lit it slowly. He inhaled and blew a cloud of smoke. 'If I knew them answers, I'd not be here, Matt. I'd be

14

after the bustard.'

'Why would anyone try to shoot you?'

Cap cocked his head to one side and grinned irritatingly. 'Why would anyone pester my little old hoss ranch, Matt? Cut fences, run my stallions into the hills, muddy up water holes?'

'Since when?'

'Since a month ago,' the old man said.

'Look, Cap, if you'd come for help once in a while . . .'

'Why?' the old man asked reasonably. 'There's no harm done Monk or Ross or me can't fix.'

'There almost was tonight.'

'Almost,' Cap admitted. 'And that's why I'm here. I want to put up some bail.'

Matt Millard snorted. 'You don't need bail for Monk, Cap. He's only in here on your say-so anyway. It was Ross that started the fight.'

'Monk, hell,' Cap said. 'Leave him get some rest. It's Ross I want.'

The sheriff shook his head. 'Ross is in for the night, maybe longer. Get yourself another poker partner.'

'Matt, any citizen can get out of this jail by posting bail, unless he's a killer. Any man but your son.'

'He's your hired hand, but he's my son. I'll judge what's best for him, Cap.'

The old man's bright eyes glittered shrewdly. 'The law is impartial, Matt.'

15

It was Matt Millard's greatest point of pride. He said now, almost stiffly, 'Always. You know I never favored Ross.'

Cap Mills cackled. 'Then you ain't got any call to disfavor him either, Matt. Now set that bail.'

Matt Millard drummed his fingers on the desk top and glared at the old man. 'What do you aim to do?'

'I aim,' Cap Mills said, 'to see about honing some of the rough edges off him. If it wasn't for that temper and that I-don't-give-a-damn-for-anything attitude of his, Ross'd be a real credit to this community.'

Matt Millard grunted. 'Some say that's my fault, spoiling him when he was a kid because he had no mother. Maybe so, but I tried to bring him up to his responsibility as a citizen.'

'He's got it,' Cap Mills agreed. 'It just hasn't come to light yet, Matt. Look at it this way—Ross is a hard worker. He's smart. He knows more about horses than I'll ever know. And I been handling 'em for nearly sixty years now. He loves that place of mine and the work it needs. But without being driven he don't do much but fool around. I'm no man to drive another. I like things too easy. So maybe some of it's my fault.'

'Is it yours or mine that he'd rather spend his time racing horses, gambling, and chasing that Bruce woman than settle down?'

Cap's mouth tightened. 'Eden Bruce is a

fine girl, Matt Millard. Don't go getting ideas from Helene Colson.'

Millard brushed Eden Bruce aside with a wave of his hand. 'There's another case— Helene. Why doesn't Ross marry her and take to running her business as she wants? My God, Cap, a handsome woman like that and they been crazy about one another since they were kids and all he wants to do is work enough for you to make a few dollars to bet on a horse race. I tell you, a spell in jail—'

'Has never done him any good,' Cap finished. He stood up. 'I been thinking about this for quite a while, Matt. I made up my mind Ross is coming out of that cell tonight. Do I have to break him out?'

Matt Millard looked at the old man and got to his feet. 'All right, Cap. As far as I'm concerned, you can take him home on the loop end of a rope behind a running horse.'

'He's man enough,' Cap Mills said. 'The only thing is he never stopped playing long enough to realize it.'

Matt Millard shrugged and went back to the small cell block behind his office. He returned with Ross, looking sleepy and battered.

'You're paroled to Cap,' Matt Millard said. 'See if you can't keep out of trouble for a while.'

'Let's go, boy,' Cap Mills said.

Ross rubbed the sleep out of his eyes. 'It's Monk's job to go for those horses. They're penned at the way station fifteen miles downtrail. Let *him* do it.'

Cap said, 'I forgot them horses. Matt, let Monk out, will you? I'll send Riley Smart along with him and they can finish that drive. I'll go for Riley right now.'

Cap and Ross walked out together, down the board sidewalk, to the livery where Riley Smart slept the remains of his life away. He wasn't eager to lift his old bones into a saddle at this time of night but five dollars sounded too good and so he saddled up and rode toward the jailhouse.

Cap led Ross toward the hotel. The old man kept a room there and had since he could remember, despite his dislike of John Colson and his daughter. He lighted a lamp, went to the dresser and brought out cards, a half-filled bottle and a box of battered poker chips. These he set on a small table.

'Let's play a few hands, Ross.'

'Is that what you got me out of jail for?'

'Can you think of a better reason?'

Ross sat down and picked up the cards. Something in the way Cap Mills spoke told him that this wasn't going to be an ordinary game.

'Cut for deal,' he said quietly.

They played two hands of poker with Ross taking both, and then three more with Cap winning each pot. There was no money riding on the game.

Ross said impatiently, 'Get to it, Cap. Two-handed poker for no stakes isn't fun for anybody.'

Cap Mills rubbed his clean-shaven cheeks with thin fingers. 'Ross, it looks like I'm going to need some help.'

Ross was silent. He took a sip of his whiskey and set down the glass. 'Cap, you never asked for help in your life.'

'I don't believe in it,' Cap Mills admitted. 'But maybe I'm getting old. I got shot at tonight.' He snorted at himself. 'Only winged the bustard, too. He missed me.'

Ross was puzzled. 'Why would anyone take a shot at you?'

Cap chuckled and gulped his drink. 'You figure I ain't worth anything? Maybe I ain't, but we know my land is—to someone.'

Ross said sourly, 'So it seems. Monk and I haven't been doing anything for the last month but fix fence and haul cayuses out of bogs.' He had a lot of Cap's philosophy in him, and since the old man had been willing to ride along and let whoever had been annoying them peck away, Ross followed suit. But the continual sniping had begun to get on his nerves.

'Cap, what have you got on the M-in-C that anyone would want that bad?' He tossed away his cigarette. 'You've got some nice meadow, a good creek, some fair draws—but nothing anybody else can't buy anywhere in these mountains.'

'Hell, I ain't,' Cap said. 'I got me more good wasteland than any man in Washington Territory.'

Ross grunted. Cap Mills being land poor was a standing joke in the Keeler country. He had bought up, one way and another, a large slice of the desert that stretched from the foot of the bench on which his land lay south-eastward. No one, including Cap himself, was sure how many acres he had accumulated, and no one, including Cap, was sure what had been his purpose in buying it. Cap always said vaguely that someday he would find a use for it. But as far as Ross could tell, it did nothing but sit there and bake in the summer and swirl with skiffs of snow in the winter and pile up taxes, small though they were. The creeks that joined at the town turned westward for the Columbia, not coming near the desert that was around the shoulder of the mountain east from Keeler, and the big creek Cap depended on dropped out of sight when it reached the dry basin. No water witch nor fancy drilling rig had ever tapped a trace of it beyond the edge of the timber.

'Go on,' Ross said. 'You haven't said it all.'

Cap dealt as he talked, recounting their annoyances on the ranch. Finally he said, 'Ross, I'm getting old and tired. I been here nearly thirty years, longer'n anyone else. I figure on going to Seattle or Portland where it's warmer in the winter. I was hoping maybe you'd lease the place from me.'

Ross was reaching for a card and his hand paused in mid-air. 'On what, Cap?'

'Meaning you don't want the responsibility, boy?'

Ross flushed. 'There's no future in it, Cap. A horse does the same thing all year around.'

Cap laughed at him. 'Now you're quoting Helene Colson, Ross. Maybe there's more future in running a hotel and a store and having your money loaned out to every businessman in Keeler and you sitting back drawing in profits. But I can't see Ross Millard sitting in an office watching his belly grow.'

'Helene knows how I feel about that,' Ross said. 'I like things the way they are.'

'But I don't,' Cap reminded him. 'And it's some different when a man is running his own place.' His shrewd eyes watched Ross a moment and then he flipped the last cards out and reached for his hand. 'Well?'

Ross fanned his cards and pushed a blue chip forward. 'I open.'

Cap stayed. 'That ain't answering my question,' he said. He made his discard. 'How many?'

Ross threw aside two and picked up a pair of treys. Cap took three. Ross said, 'I'll bet two blues. Cap, you've never meddled in my affairs before. Why now?'

The old man spat a fleck of tobacco from his lip. 'Now you think I'm like some I could name around here—wanting to make a man out of you. I raise a yellow.'

Ross called, then said, 'I've heard that since I was a kid. My life is my own. Let me live it.'

Cap showed his hand. Two pair. Ross had three treys and took the pot. Cap said, 'There's only three people in this town who will let you alone, boy. Me and your friends at the Big Hat. But that ain't here or there. I asked a straight question and I want a straight answer. I'll change it. You want to buy the ranch?'

'No.'

'Then deal.' Ross dealt and they let the cards lie. Cap said, 'Or lease the ranch?'

'No.'

Ross was puzzled again and a little wary. He knew the old man well enough to be sure that if he had his mind set on Ross running the ranch, somehow Ross would end up doing just that.

Cap said, 'Then I'll make you a bet—if you're still a gambling man.'

Ross thought, This is what he's been working up to. He said, 'Name it.'

'We deal a hand of showdown,' Cap said carefully. 'If you win, you work for me for a year. No horse racing, no going off catting anymore'n a regular workman does—a Saturday night now and then. But work to build up my place, fix the breeding stock, clean up the pastures, increase the herd, make the place worth something again. I been lazy too long and it's shoddy now.'

'If I win, I do that?' Ross laughed. 'What happens if I lose?'

'If you lose, you get the ranch, lock, stock, and barrel—and title.'

Ross thought for a minute that Cap had gone foolish on him. Then he said, 'Cap, do you have any relatives?'

'Nope.'

'Did you ever make a will?'

'Yep. And left everything to you, whether you like it or not.'

Ross flushed, though he had suspected this before. He said, 'What if I up and sold the place?'

'Your privilege,' Cap said. 'If you lose the bet and get the ranch, it's yours to do as you damn please with. No strings. If I get shot, same thing. All the difference is, I'm retiring instead of dying—if I win this pot.'

'Ah,' Ross said, 'then the bets are for you, not me.'

'Hell,' Cap snorted, 'a man always looks to himself first.'

'Who gets the profits I build up if I win and have to fix your ranch?'

'You do,' Cap said. 'After a year I'll get the place back all fancied up, run it down again because I'm lazy, and leave it to you in my will.' He cackled. 'The more fixing you do, the more profit you make, and the less run down it'll be when I die.'

'You won't die for twenty years,' Ross said. He could see Cap's angle. The old man was betting all in favor of himself from one point of view—if he won, he'd have his freedom and be rid of the ranch he intended to give to Ross someday anyway. If he lost, he'd have a year of freedom and the place all fixed up when he came back. Then he probably had it in his mind to work Ross into taking over to reap the benefit of the efforts he would have put in. He knew the old man would enjoy just this kind of bet, thinking himself clever for having thought it up.

But maybe Cap wasn't as clever as he thought. Win or lose, Ross knew that he could fix the ranch up in a year. If he just got that year's profit, he would have a nice piece of change and he could use the time to breed himself some racing stock, besides. If he owned the ranch, he could sell it any time he wished.

He said, 'Who deals this bet, Cap?'

Cap picked up the hand Ross had dealt and neither had looked at. 'Let's take this one. Since you dealt with no real stakes, there's no question of hornswoggling.'

Ross spread his hand out, three deuces and a pair of nines for a full house. Cap lifted his tufted eyebrows in suprise and then glanced at his own cards. He flipped them down one at a time, and Ross found himself staring at four jacks.

'Looks like you dealt yourself a ranch that time,' Cap said, and cackled.

If Ross hadn't known the old man so well, he would have suspected some kind of trick. But no one had ever accused Cap Mills of playing anything but a straight hand. He said, 'All right, Cap. It's mine—no strings.'

'No strings.' Cap got up and walked to a dresser, brought out a pen and bottle of ink and a sheet of paper. He trimmed the pen carefully and then wrote in his big scrawl on the paper. He handed it to Ross when the ink was dry.

Ross read slowly, working to make out the poorly written words:

*I, Cap Mills, hereby turn over my entir property, lock stok, barrell, and title—and trouble therwith—to Ross Millard to have and to hold and to do with what he damn well pleases. Dated this 13th day of May, 1887. Signed, Cap Mills*

Ross folded the paper and tucked it into the inside band of his hat. Cap nodded. 'All right. Now I got to get home so's I can pack my duffel. I'll take tomorrow's stage to Pinkney City and then it's Seattle for the old man.' He cackled at Ross. 'That's a real weight off my shoulders. Now you and Monk worry alone about the cut fence and such.'

'You're a liar,' Ross said sourly. He clapped his hat on his head and walked out, closing the door not too quietly behind himself. Cap Mills chuckled, plucked a few cards from his sleeve and prepared to leave.

As Ross went through the lobby, he glanced at the little room behind the desk where Helene had her outer office. She was bent over a desk, working on her books. He rapped on the glass panel of the door.

Helene lifted her head, showing him the softness of her profile. Her china-blue eyes lighted and she waved a hand at him. He opened the door and entered.

'I thought you were on your way to river,' she said. 'Then I heard you were in jail and then—'

'And then?'

'And here you are.' She laughed a little breathlessly, a half-suppressed sound. 'I've been feeling neglected.'

'I can't compete with a set of books,' he said. He lifted one of her ink-smudged fingers and glared at it. Too often he remembered asking Helene for her company only to find the books between them.

'Well,' she said, 'if I had a helper, this could get done in the daytime.' She saw his set expression and added, 'I talked to the new dealer at the saloon. He's been an accountant and I just might hire him for this job.'

'Good idea,' Ross said indifferently. He

grimaced. 'Sorry, Helene. But I just bought myself a load of responsibility. And one is enough for the time being.'

She sat down again, smoothing back her silk-blonde hair. She was not a tall woman, but she was gracefully proportioned and aware that her beauty was equally apparent seated or standing.

'You bought—what?'

'I won,' he amended, 'Cap's ranch.' He told her about the deal. 'So I can sell at a fair price when I get it fixed up.'

The frown on her face surprised him. She said, 'Sell—to whom?'

He shrugged. 'Someone wants it badly enough now to push the old man around. If I wait long enough, an offer will be made, I think.'

She said slowly, 'How do you know you can fix it up—if someone is causing all this trouble?'

He said, almost awkwardly, 'Cap was right, I guess. Now that it's mine, I'm not going to let myself be pushed around. I can stop it, Helene.'

'Be careful, Ross!'

Startled, he glanced at her, but she had looked away. 'You sound as if you think there's danger.'

'Isn't there—from someone who would treat an old man that way?'

'I suppose so,' he agreed. He rose and took his hat. 'Anyway, if you want a temporary ranch owner for a husband, that's one thing. But a bookkeeper—you'd best see Chet Walsh over at the saloon. Just don't let him deal you a crooked deck.'

She got up and went to the door with him, holding him with a hand over his that rested on the latch. 'Ross, what's happened to us? We used to think nothing in the world was as important as our getting married. Then—well, is it that Bruce girl?'

Ross looked down into her face. He said, 'Eden Bruce is a nice girl. I like her. But—no, it isn't that, Helene. I think it's just what you and everyone else have been saying. I don't like responsibility. A wife is certainly that.'

She forced a smile. 'I'll keep trying.' She lifted a hand on which a small diamond glittered. 'You see, I've regarded myself as engaged ever since you gave it to me.'

'Kid stuff,' Ross blurted. 'You know I won it at a race five years ago.' He saw the hurt on her features and added, 'I'd like to get you a real one when the time comes.'

'When the time comes,' she murmured. 'Always when—never now.' She stepped back. 'Come over to the house some night, Ross. It's lonesome.'

He nodded and walked out, less satisfied than ever. He did not know what he had expected, telling Helene what he had. He didn't even know, really, how he felt about her. Sometimes when they were more alone than a glass-paneled door allowed and she gave him her lips and the pressure of her body and the fine, sweet smell of her hair, with all the promises that lay in her caress, he thought he was a fool for putting off their marriage any longer. And then, when he saw her like this, working, he knew that the driving nature that had made her father rich was in her, too, and she would never let him rest from making money, something that to him meant only a means of finding pleasure.

He scowled as he stepped into the night air and started for the saloon.

He thought, As soon as Cap leaves, I'll go to work and fix up the place and get it in shape for a sale. It'll bring a nice piece of change and . . . The words in his mind dwindled away. Cap's had been the gamble, after all, he realized. He had taken the chance Ross wouldn't be low enough to sell him out.

'Why,' he said aloud, 'he really did euchre me!' He stomped into the Big Hat and up to the nearly empty bar. 'By God,' he said, 'I'll show that old sharper he can't get away with his tricks. I'll shove his ranch back down his throat!'

# CHAPTER THREE

Eden Bruce was seated at Rube Overman's table, sipping coffee and eating a late bite, when Ross came in.

Overman said in his soft voice, 'Ross looks mad again. I wonder what it is this time.'

Eden set down her cup and rose. 'I'll go find out,' she said. 'I don't want him getting in jail twice in the same night.'

'She can't nursemaid him forever,' Overman said to himself. Through sleepy-looking eyes, be watched as Eden reached the bar.

Ross was sipping a beer, glowering from it to the big bar mirror now and then, not moving except to pick up his glass, hunched over the bar with his shoulders forward like a man about to charge into something. He was not aware of Eden until she stopped alongside of him and spoke.

'Troubles again?'

He glanced her way and his frown smoothed out. Eden usually had that effect on him.

Now, studying her, he knew that this night she was someone he could talk to. His smile was thin but it contained his thanks.

He said, 'More troubles than usual, Eden.'

'You wouldn't want to tell me about it— before you bite the rim from that glass?'

He nodded, took his beer and followed her

to a table. She had a waiter bring her food over and then sat quietly, eating and listening to him talk. He outlined what Cap had done and mentioned his talk with Helene.

She said carefully, 'Why don't you marry her, Ross? She's beautiful, gracious . . .'

He emptied his glass and thudded it on the table. 'And be her bookkeeper for the rest of my life?'

'That isn't the reason she'd marry you,' Eden said. 'No woman would marry a man just for a business partner.'

'Especially this man,' he said, and smiled crookedly. 'You're a good friend, Eden. It's a relief to be able to talk to someone who understands.'

'A good friend,' she murmured, and turned her eyes to her coffee cup. 'I'll try to understand,' she said.

'But I didn't come in here to talk to you about Helene. It's the ranch.'

'The ranch—you mean the trouble Cap's been having?'

'No. I mean the troubles I've got. I won the ranch from Cap tonight.' Ross glowered into his empty glass.

'Well, what are you going to do about it?' Eden asked reasonably.

'Do?' he said. 'I don't like to be hoodwinked, not even by Cap Mills. I'm going to give him back the place before he gets on that stage. If he wants me to work for him, fine. If not, that's fine, too.'

She studied this. Then she said, 'Have another beer, Ross.' She signaled the bartender, who raised his eyebrows in surprise at the signal, shrugged, and fixed the beer. Ross accepted it and drank a deep gulp. 'You think the same thing—I'm afraid of the responsibility?'

'I didn't say that.'

'I'm not,' he said. He stopped and thought it over. 'If Cap hadn't double-dealt on me, maybe I'd—' He stopped again, this time to smother a yawn. 'Guess I'm sleepy.' He got up, reached for the beer and finished it, and then smiled down at her with an effort. 'I'll bunk in Cap's room at the hotel so I can be close to the stage when he takes it.'

'If he takes it,' Eden said. Ross yawned again, sat down heavily in the chair, put his head on the table, and went soundly to sleep.

She signaled to Rube Overman and Potsy, the waiter. 'Ross seems to have drunk too much,' she said to Rube, avoiding the steady look he gave her. 'Shall we get him to bed in the spare room? If we take him across to the hotel, there'll be talk again.'

The bartender and Potsy maneuvered Ross up the stairs to a small room next to Overman's office. They laid him on the bed, as Overman directed, and then left, shutting the door quietly. Eden had followed them, bringing Ross's hat, and now she tossed it to a chair.

'Let's get his shirt and boots off, at least, Rube.'

Rube grunted, working on the boots. 'I saw your signal, Eden . . . What was he thinking of doing, killing someone?'

'No,' she said quietly. 'He won Cap Mills' ranch in a card game tonight. Cap set it up for him to win so that he can go to the coast. Ross wants to give it back to him.'

'Makes life complicated, doesn't it,' Rube said dryly, 'when a man has to be responsible for a few thousand acres and a couple thousand head of horse stock?' He set the boots down. 'Do you think you can make him keep the place this way?'

'It's worth a try,' she said. 'We'll see.'

Overman tossed a blanket over Ross. 'Maybe I should give him two blankets, now that he's a big property owner.' They went out quietly, taking the lamp with them. Ross slept without moving.

Downstairs, Overman said seriously, 'Are you sure that Ross didn't want Cap's place? Maybe he's the one who's been doing the fence cutting and such just to drive the old man away. And if, as you say, he dealt that hand of cards . . .'

'You think that of Ross Millard?'

Overman held up sausage-shaped fingers and counted them off. 'Remember, Cap loves that ranch. It's hard to picture him losing it.

33

And Ross might be tired of this ragging he takes all the time.'

'Ross could always marry Helene,' she said bitterly.

'If he does, he's not the man I take him for.' Overman got up slowly. 'I'm just telling you what the town will say to this, Eden. It might have been better to let him give the place back to Cap. There'll be talk—mean talk. There always is.'

'But if Cap tells the way it was before he takes the stage—'

Overman nodded. 'I'll ride out in the morning and see him about it,' he said. 'I think Ross is telling the truth; maybe I can put a little weight behind his story.' With a nod, he went upstairs.

*       *       *

Ross slept heavily until shortly before dawn. Then, the drug worn off, he awakened, sat up, startled. His head hurt like the devil and his throat was dry. He couldn't place where he was until he had struck a match and looked around. Then he shook his head, wincing at the pain it sent through his skull.

'Two beers?' he muttered. Or was it two beers? He couldn't remember. He lay back down and tried to piece things together. Then, as they came slowly back, be realized it had been two beers.

34

'Friends,' he groaned. The only answer could be that his last beer had been doped. The purpose of it was slow in coming to him until, turning Eden's talk over in his mind, it struck him that she hadn't wanted him to turn the ranch back to Cap.

Another phrase of hers came back to him. 'If Cap takes the stage.'

With a groan, Ross sat up and felt for his boots. He got them on, put on his shirt and vest, found his hat and pushed it on his head and then stumbled for the door. He went down the stairs as quietly as he could and out the rear door to where he had left his horse. It was a half-broke animal, one of the herd he had been pushing when his own mount went lame. By the time it was under control, his head felt swollen and ready to burst, with pain pounding his eyeballs. He wanted nothing so much as a drink of water. The whole thing brought back his anger at Cap Mills and Eden.

He rode south out of town, cutting east toward the mountains and then north onto Cap Mills' benchland. When he came to the creek, he stopped long enough to bury his face in the icy water, sucking in great draughts to cool his head and stomach until he became sick. After that was over, he felt better. He drank a few more swallows and mounted again.

He rode on, yawning wearily, holding the fractious horse down in the blackness of predawn. He judged he was close to an old line shack just off the trail and that meant Cap's house was only a short way ahead. He pushed the horse a little, eager to get to the old man. Suddenly he felt the animal pitch on him as though it had stepped into a gopher hole. He reached for the horn, missed as the horse went to its knees, and catapulted over its head onto the hard-packed dirt of the trail. There was a sensation of a sudden gush of air leaving his body and then he lost consciousness.

\*      \*      \*

When the last customer left the Big Hat, Chet Walsh stood up from the green cloth-covered table and began to gather his equipment. He heard someone coming toward him and he lifted his head and looked into the steady dark eyes of Eden Bruce.

'Hello, little sweetheart,' he said softly. 'This is a very profitable place you have here.'

'Don't call me that!' she said fiercely.

The smile on his lean, handsome face was mocking. 'I have no intention of revealing our secret, Miss Bruce.' His voice was dry. 'If you don't choose to admit our relationship, why should I?'

'Former relationship,' she said tartly. 'I didn't ask you to come here, Chet. You followed me. It was a peaceful year until you came.' She leaned on the table, looking almost pleadingly at him. 'As an eighteen-year-old girl, it was romantic running off with a gambler. It wasn't so romantic after I found marriage was only a word to him and—'

'And?'

'And that he didn't know the meaning of the word honest. I spent too many years running from you not to think you came here for a purpose. What is it?'

'A man just might get tired of the old ways, Eden.'

'In anyone else I could believe it,' she said. 'In you, never. And I warn you, any of your tricks and—'

He was a strong man for all his slenderness, and now he lifted a pack of cards in one hand and squeezed them to shapelessness. 'And you'll turn me in?'

She ignored his implied warning. 'Rather than have you ruin people as you have before, yes.'

'And then the story would come out. How would that set with Overman?'

'My life before I came here is no concern of his.'

'And Ross Millard,' he said mockingly.

'Chet, I'm warning—' She broke off, feeling the helplessness she always did when she tried to face him down. She knew that here was persecution she might never escape from this side of death. Even the fact that she could always send him East with a word to any law officer, send him for trial and possibly to prison, was no consolation. To turn him in was not in Eden Bruce's make-up.

'Why don't you go keep Helene Colson's books, Chet? And leave me alone.'

He laughed at her. 'Maybe I will—when she needs me desperately enough. Right now I like my job.'

'If I ever hear of one accusation, Chet, one bad deal—'

'Have you ever seen me cheat here, sweetheart? I'm an honest dealer—it's safer that way.'

She left him, fighting tears as she heard his soft laughter.

Walsh got his hat and went into the night. There were no lights showing in Keeler now except for the soft one in the hotel lobby, no sound but the echo of his own footsteps on the board sidewalk. He hesitated before the hotel and then went past the alley to see if there was a light in the big house set at the foot of the hills that backed the town.

There was, a single faint glow, nearly muffled by curtains, and he knew that Helene Colson was expecting him. A sophisticated woman, this, he thought. And yet not too sophisticated. At first, he had assumed that a young and beautiful woman in business would be easy to pick clean. Then he found that under the softness and the beauty was a hard core of resistance where money was concerned.

Walsh had made it a point to look over the country, to seek what would be the best opportunity not only for quick money but big and lasting money. Only that, he knew, would tempt a person like Helene Colson. And after he found such a situation, the rest had been easily and skillfully done.

He reached the house and let himself in the side door, found his way through the blackness of the parlor and slipped up the stairs to where lamplight showed beneath a door. He eased back the latch and entered.

Helene was seated by a table on which some ledger sheets were laid. A coffee pot and two cups were beside her, and when she saw Walsh, she poured both cups full.

'This is fresh,' she said. 'You're late tonight.'

He took the coffee and drew a chair near her. She was dressed as she had been earlier, in a deep-green gown that set off the loveliness of her blonde hair. Her beauty struck Walsh afresh and he crushed down an impulse to go to her and catch her in his arms.

'Meeting like this,' she said, 'makes me feel cheap. As if—'

'No one knows,' he said quietly. 'And you know that it isn't "as if . . ."'

Helene studied him, his lean, dark handsomeness, the thin line of mustache over the bold mouth, the dark eyes beneath heavy brows, the black hair. She held no illusions as to his intent, and at the times when Ross seemed particularly out of reach, she was almost tempted to accept Chet Walsh. But on her own terms. She said, 'It would make things a lot easier if you'd go to work for me, Chet. Especially now.'

'Why especially now?'

She said, 'Cap Mills lost his ranch to Ross tonight gambling. Ross claims Cap bet so that Ross got the ranch for *losing* a poker hand. Anyway, Cap is going to the coast and Ross has title. I saw it.'

Walsh set down his coffee cup. 'So Millard is the M-in-C now. That might change things.' His eyes were on her shrewdly, knowing how she felt about Ross.

'He wants to fix it up and sell,' she said. 'Maybe we can get him to sell before he fixes it up. That would be the easiest way. Then we could stop all this—'

'Or we could cut enough more fence and muddy enough water holes to make him sell,' Walsh said quickly.

'I know Ross,' she said warningly. 'It's his place now. Whether he wants it or not, he'll fight for it.'

'He might get shot,' Walsh murmured.

She winced. 'That would throw the property into litigation and we might not get it for years. There'll be no bloodshed.'

'I feel the same way.'

Helene drummed her fingers on the table

40

top. 'What about the shooting of Cap Mills?'

'Sweeney missed him purposely,' Walsh told her. 'But Mills winged Sweeney. It was just another move, that's all.'

'There'll be no more of them,' Helene said. 'And I say to call off your men. Worrying Cap Mills was one thing; trying it on Ross Millard is another. We'll approach him on a sale.'

'And if he refuses?'

'Then,' she said, 'is the time to think of something else.' She rose. 'I know these people here, Chet. I know how far they can be pushed. The stakes are too big to stumble now.'

Walsh nodded. He was the one who had visualized those stakes. Perhaps everyone in Keeler had been too close to things to see the possibilities that lay in the creek on Cap Mills' ranch. For it started on his land and ended on it and was snow- and spring-fed and grown almost to a river by the time it disappeared into the desert. But somehow it had never occurred to anyone to dam the creek and turn water on the desert. He had described it in glowing terms to Helene the first time—the farmers that they could sell the land to once it was irrigated, the growth of the town, the profits from the land as well as those from the town. And with a few careful moves, once the property was obtained, she could buy up land that would become valuable when Keeler boomed.

It was a handsome picture, well painted by Walsh. He pointed out beyond the immediate goal, the reminder that the territory would soon become a state. That meant politics, and a wealthy man, backed by a wealthy woman, could go far. He skipped the capital at Olympia, picturing for her the society at Washington, D.C., the glitter, the sophistication, the great people who came there from all the capitals of the world. He had little talking to do.

Now he said only, 'There'll be no stumbling. Your plan is sensible. We'll try it first.'

He went to the hotel, first to his own room and then to one farther along the hall, where he rapped sharply before returning to his room. Soon a man came, shutting the door behind him.

Walsh lighted a cigar, poured himself a drink, and waved a hand at the bottle. 'Things have changed,' he said. 'The order is to lay off the M-in-C. You can ride out tomorrow, Pickett, and tell the boys.'

Pickett took a deep drink. He was a small man, scrawny but wiry, who wore a gun that looked too big for him. He sat down now and said, 'Monk rode out for Mills' horses. Why not do something about it?'

'And have Monk suspected? No, thanks,' Walsh said. 'You're a fool. So is Sweeney, letting an old man shoot him.' He dragged on his cigar. 'Millard won the old man's ranch and the old man is heading for Seattle. We'll see that he doesn't get there. He can take his rest up at the timber camp where the boys are. We go tonight and we make it look good—for us. And bad for Millard.'

'Where is Millard?'

'Sleeping one off at the Big Hat,' Walsh said. 'Let's ride.'

Pickett brought a pair of horses from the barn at the rear of the hotel and they mounted, starting southward in the darkness. They had gone only a short way when Walsh stopped.

'Rider coming.'

They waited until they saw Ross Millard on his fractious horse go slowly by. Walsh said, 'If I know Millard, he'll be going up to give the place back to the old man. You cut over the hump and get him off his horse before he gets there.'

'What with—my gun?'

'Don't be a fool!' Walsh said sharply. 'Did you see how he rode? He's still half out. Trip the horse. If it doesn't throw him, use your gun butt. Put him in that old line shack this side of Mills' place. He'll wake up and never know the difference. Think he was thrown.'

Pickett took off, cutting up a steep trail that broke onto the bench much more quickly than the longer wagon road. Walsh trailed Ross, going slowly. He reached a point near the line shack in time to see Pickett wind up the rope

43

he had stretched across the trail. Ross lay in a heap on the ground, motionless.

'Out cold,' Pickett said. 'Fell on his shoulder and knocked the wind out.'

'Hurry it,' Walsh ordered. Together they got Ross to the line shack and threw him on an ancient bunk there. Then they left, riding the remaining distance to Cap Mills' M-in-C at a lope.

Walsh let out a sigh of relief when he saw a light coming from the window. Together they slipped on foot to the house. Through the window, they could see Cap packing a suitcase, stopping now and then to drink some of his early-morning coffee. Occasionally he would laugh out loud.

Walsh made a sign to Pickett, who went back to his horse, mounted, and rode it forward loudly. Cap Mills cocked his head and then moved toward the door. It came open, spilling light into the yard and framing him.

'Who's there? Who's riding?'

'Over here,' Walsh called softly.

Cap swung that way. Pickett was off his horse now, in shadow. 'No, this way, Mills.'

'Over here,' Walsh said again. 'This way, Mills.'

Cap swung back, dragging his gun from its holster. The swish of a rope was gentle on the chill air. He cursed as it settled over him, pinning his arms, trapping his gun halfway out of the holster. The gun fell to the ground, leaving him empty-handed, standing hatless in the square of light.

'I'll take him,' Walsh said softly to Pickett. 'You do the rest here. And see that you make it look good. I think this time when Millard goes to jail, he'll stay a while—on suspicion of murder.'

## CHAPTER FOUR

Rube Overman heaved his bulk out of his buggy and walked heavily up to Cap Mills' front door. It stood open and he could see a man moving inside in the dimness.

Overman stopped in the doorway, his hand lifted to rap. He let the hand fall. It was Ross Millard and he was walking around dazedly, looking here and there as if he had lost something.

' 'Morning,' Rube said.

Ross whirled around and then relaxed as he saw who it was. 'I'm looking for Cap,' he said. Overman came in. The big parlor was cool, almost cold, as if there had been no fire in the stove that morning. There no smell of breakfast lingering on the air.

Overman asked, 'Has he been home?'

'He said he was coming here last night,' Ross said. He looked weary, his face drawn.

'Maybe he's already packed and gone,'

Overman suggested.

'So I thought,' Ross agreed. 'His clothes are gone from the bedroom; so is his suitcase, that old leather one he used so long.' He shook his head. 'But if he figured on being gone for a year or better, he wouldn't go off and leave that old gun of his.' He pointed to the mantel where an old rifle hung on pegs above the fireplace. 'He killed too many Indians with that one to leave it, Rube.'

Overman pulled at his heavy lower lip. 'What are you getting at, Ross?'

'There are tracks in the yard,' Ross said. 'Two riders were here not too long ago.' He sniffed. 'There's gunsmoke still on the air in here. There are the things that Cap didn't take with him.' He pointed at the table. 'And there's the cup of coffee he didn't finish.' He walked across the floor slowly and pointed to where the wood along the edge of the rug showed fresh scrubbing. He touched a finger to it. 'That's still damp. It's soft wood and what was cleaned up didn't all come out. It's blood, Rube.'

Rube Overman found a chair and lowered himself into it. Ross said, 'We were being hoorawed here, 'you know. And last night someone tried to shoot Cap.'

'I heard,' Overman said quietly. 'Go on.'

'It looks to me like someone got over-eager in trying to run him out of here.'

'So it does. But why?'

46

Ross rolled and lighted a cigarette. 'I'll be the one to find out why, I suppose, as soon as the news gets circulated that I own the place.'

'The whole town will know it soon enough,' Rube told him. 'Did you come this morning to take possession, Ross?'

'I came to give it back,' Ross retorted sharply.

'It would sell for a good price.'

'You know Cap euchred me into this as his way of preaching at me. I wanted to give it back. I'll live my own life the way I see fit.'

'That I doubt,' Overman told him.

'Meaning what?'

'Look,' Overman said, 'you left my place about three this morning. I heard you go. Who's to say whether you came to give the place back or whether you came to make sure he didn't try to take it back? It's quite a thing for a man to have Cap Mills' M-in-C ranch.' There was no censure, no accusation, on Overman's round face.

'So that's the way it'll be.'

'That's the way it'll be,' Rube Overman agreed. 'You know this town as well as I do, Ross. It's what they'll say. It's what the—the sheriff will believe.'

Ross was silent, twisting it over in his mind. Overman said, 'Maybe that's the way it's supposed to look, Ross.'

'If Cap was killed to get at me—'

'You get the ranch easier, maybe,' Overman

47

said. 'You're just part of it, I'd say.'

A rider was coming fast across the meadow. Ross went to the door and looked out. 'It's Monk,' he said

'Your hired hand,' Overman said dryly.

Monk came in truculently, his eyes suspicious at the sight of Overman in Cap Mills' parlor. Overman was notorious for never stirring for anything short of war or famine.

'Where's Cap? Them danged horses—'

'I think he went to Seattle,' Overman said quickly.

Monk swung on him. 'He didn't tell me he was going anywhere.'

'Nor me,' Overman agreed complacently. 'But that was before he lost the ranch in a card game.'

Before Monk could say anything, Overman nodded to Ross, and Ross showed the title to Monk, who read it and thrust it aside. 'So now I'm working for you?'

It was on the tip of Ross's tongue to tell him to pack up and go, but he stopped. Monk Ryker was a top workman for all his truculence and hatred of Ross Millard. He said, 'It seems so,' and let it go at that.

Monk walked through the house and came back, stopping before Overman and glaring at him. 'I don't like this. The old man wouldn't leave in the middle of the night. Where would he go?'

'Maybe he went to the hotel to wait for the stage. Maybe he rode over the hump to Pinkney City. How would I know?'

Monk looked at Ross. 'When did you get here?'

Ross ignored the demand in Monk's voice. 'About a half hour ago. Ask Rube where I was last night.'

'Sleeping it off at my place,' Rube Overman said dryly. 'Eden and I put him to bed.'

Monk swung around and stomped out of the house to his horse. He lifted the reins and led it toward the barn.

Ross folded up the tide and replaced it in his hatband. He could see the position he was in. Monk's attitude was almost as if he had sensed something wrong. The town would have a field day. His father . . .

He thought, I could sell out and leave the country.

It came to him suddenly and so hard that there was no room for argument in his mind. He could go nowhere, do nothing until he found what had happened to Cap Mills. Not just for his own sake but for Cap's. If, he thought, he was free long enough to do anything at all.

\*       \*       \*

Ross worked his way along the narrow path that led from Cap Mills' ranch house through

49

the bole-to-bole timber westward to the wagon road. The tracks he had seen in the yard had told him a good deal at first. Two horses had ridden in slowly, then one had gone at a run. They had left at different times, the first man leading another horse at a slow, steady gait, and the second a good hour or more behind, coming at a swift clip.

The sign also told Ross that the riders had taken the cut-off path across Cap's flatland where it bordered on the wagon road. But there he lost the trail.

Whoever it had been had been careful once the wagon road was reached. He had no way of knowing whether they had ridden up toward the hump or down toward town. Dissatisfied and irritated, he returned to the ranch.

That evening after supper, he took out pencil and paper and listed the things he felt should be changed about the place. Cap had grown lazy the last few years. Many things that could have been profitably expanded had been put off. Totaling them up, Ross saw a good year's work for two or even three men.

He was folding the paper when he heard a rider coming. Reaching up, he took his gun from the peg on the wall and stood listening.

There was the creak of leather as someone left the saddle, then the thump of heavy boots on the steps.

His father entered, wide and solid.

'I heard,' he said.

Ross indicated a chair and went to the stove to get the sheriff a cup of coffee. 'Rube tell you?'

Matt Millard nodded. 'Overman tells me Cap went to Seattle. He didn't catch the stage today. What did he do, ride a broomstick?'

Ross shrugged. 'Overman doesn't really think that, any more than I do—though Cap could have ridden over to Pinkney City.' He sat down, sipping his own coffee, and detailed what had happened since he left the jail.

'It's a thin story,' he said when he was done. 'I have no proof the horse threw me. I don't even remember getting to the line shack. But I awoke there and found the horse grazing by the door, loose.'

His father said, 'When you got here the old man was gone, suitcase, clothes and nothing else?'

'But like I said,' Ross told him, 'he left that gun and there's the scrubbed place on the floor.'

Matt Millard filled his pipe slowly. 'You're putting a rope around your neck, son.'

'So I know,' Ross admitted. 'I told you how I felt—how I feel. I want no part of owning this place.'

Idly Matt Millard picked up the paper Ross had worked out his plans on and scanned it. 'For a man who wants no part of it, you've done a lot of planning.'

'What else can I do?' Ross demanded. 'If

51

Cap is dead, I have a moral obligation to do what he wanted, don't I? If he's alive, that obligation holds until I can find him and give him back the place.'

'It's yours to sell,' the sheriff said.

'My concern right now is what happened to Cap.'

'Got any ideas?'

Ross told him about the tracking he had done that morning. 'I figure,' he said, 'whoever rode from here first took Cap somewhere and the other one stayed to clean up.'

'Took him—how?'

'On his own horse,' Ross said. 'Dead or alive.'

'Took him off to bury him,' Matt Millard said. 'That makes no sense, Ross. If they wanted him dead, why not just leave him?'

'That's my reason for hoping he's not dead,' Ross said. 'Look at it this way. Cap was being bothered, fences cut, you know all that. Last night someone shot at him—and missed. Then Cap turned this place over to me and this happened.'

His father said shrewdly, 'You think someone is trying to make sure you'll sell? Sell and run before a possible murder charge can be made against you?'

'It's possible.'

'That means someone knew last night, or early this morning, that you owned the place.'

'That's where I'm stumped,' Ross said.

'Helene knew, and Eden Bruce knew and Rube Overman. No one else.'

'And you say the Bruce girl fed you knockout drops?'

'I said I was with her when it happened. I don't know whose idea it was. Why would Eden . . .' His voice trailed off under the sheriff's steady stare. What did he really know about Eden Bruce?

His father rose. 'Mind if I bunk here? I want to check those tracks first thing in the morning.'

'Help yourself,' Ross said. 'Use Cap's room.' He added, 'It doesn't look like he'll be needing it for a while.'


## CHAPTER FIVE

When Matt Millard left the M-in-C around mid-morning, Ross saddled up and rode along with him. The sheriff was silent until they reached the short trail that branched off to the old line shack. He said then, 'Did you come back this way when you tried following those tracks?' Ross shook his head. 'Then,' his father said quietly, 'do it now.'

Despite the fact that Ross and his father had never been close to one another, he had always been sensitive to the older man's tone of voice. Now, in surprise, he reined in his horse and went forward on foot. There had been something gently triumphant in that voice, and even a faint tone of pleasure. It took Ross only a few moments to read the sign that led from the trail to the door and then went away again.

He looked up at his father, who had accompanied him. 'I'd say the same pair that rode into Cap's yard came in here carrying something heavy, and went out light. Those tracks there are mine—and they were made later.'

'I'd say the same thing,' the sheriff answered. 'Where do you remember falling off your horse?'

Ross showed him. The trail was chopped up by hoofs at that point; it was almost impossible to read any definite sign. At the top of the trail where it broke down onto the great stretch of wasteland, Matt Millard reined in once more.

'What has this place got that's so important? What has it got that a man with a little capital couldn't get by buying any other run-down place?' Ross could only shrug. The sheriff added, 'That . . .' and pointed to the wasteland.

'I've thought of it,' Ross admitted. 'And it adds up to nothing. It sure doesn't add up to the answer of where Cap has gone.'

'Shot and buried,' the sheriff said grimly. 'And you the man who stands to profit by it.'

'So I am,' Ross agreed quietly. 'But what

about those tracks back there? At the line shack, at Cap's place?'

'There are two answers to that,' Matt Millard said. 'Either you're telling the truth or you're in with somebody else on this.'

'You'd think that of me?'

'What I think has no meaning,' his father said. 'It's what the evidence shows. And if it comes to a trial, it's what the town thinks.'

'In other words,' Ross remarked, 'the law more than half suspects I'm guilty. According to law, I'm innocent until proved guilty, but that doesn't always work with public opinion or with the law.' He saw a flush creep over his father's face. 'So I'll have to prove my own innocence.'

'It's the law's job to find out what happened to Cap,' the sheriff said. 'I play no favorites.'

'Nor any prejudices,' Ross suggested dryly. He lifted the reins and spurred on toward town.

His first move in town was to register the title Cap had made out to him.

Marsh Whelan, the teller, vice-president, and general factotum, came to the window where Ross waited, took the title silently, and read it as quickly as Cap Mills' handwriting would permit. Looking at his face that had the set of a flint rock out of the hills, Ross was reminded of the bankers in newspaper cartoons.

'That's a lot of land,' Whelan said.

'A lot,' Ross agreed. 'But it's no more work to transfer a lot than a little.'

'It's not worth much the way Cap let it slide,' the banker said.

'I'm not in here to get an appraisal,' Ross said.

The old man's eyes lifted. 'Nor a loan?'

'Nor a loan,' he said flatly. 'You can put your money back in the vaults, Marsh.'

Marsh Whelan went away and came back with the forms needed to make the transfer. He filled out the blanks, then pushed the paper over for Ross to sign. Whelan said, 'Cap Mills was a friend of mine, Ross.'

Ross lifted his head. 'And mine, Marsh.'

'In my book, a man doesn't take advantage of his friends,' Whelan went on.

'Meaning?' It was coming, Ross thought.

'Cap always took too big a risk gambling. Most of us knew that and protected him from himself.'

'If Cap comes back, he can have the place any time.'

'You could hardly do otherwise,' Marsh Whelan agreed. 'If Cap comes back.'

Ross thrust his pen across the paper to make his signature, turned around and walked out. On the street, he paused, standing in the sunlight, shaking a little at the anger in him. More of the townspeople were going about their business as the time for midday dinner came closer. Now and then one looked curiously at him but most walked on by, without the usual familiar greeting.

Ross went down the street toward the Big Hat.

The Big Hat was dim and cool and nearly empty. Ross saw Rube Overman at his usual table, taking coffee. He paused at the bar long enough to buy a beer and get a plate of lunch, then he walked across the dance floor and sat down across from Overman.

'I heard you were in town,' Overman said. 'Maybe you'd have been wiser to stay out.'

'If someone wants the place bad enough,' Ross said, around a mouthful of beef, 'they'll come after me like they went after Cap. The sooner it's known I'm the owner, the better.'

'Trap bait,' Overman murmured. 'Have any nibbles yet?'

Ross told him about his father's visit and of the reaction of Marsh Whelan. Overman nodded. 'So you came here—?'

'To see Eden,' Ross said.

Overman rose laboriously, waddled across the room, and disappeared. Shortly, Eden Bruce came down the stairs, dressed for the street. She got a cup of coffee at the counter and then came to where Ross was finishing his meal. He rose as she approached the table. With a quick smile, she seated herself.

'Rube said you wanted to talk to me.' She hesitated. 'Ross, I'm sorry about Cap.'

'We don't know that there's anything to be

sorry for—yet,' he said. He was conscious of her beauty, of the attraction it had for him, and he knew that here he must talk without letting his feeling for her sway him.

'Why did you have me drugged the other night' he demanded flatly. 'To keep me from going to Caps, to—'

'To let someone kill him,' she finished. 'You're letting yourself form opinions just as the rest of the town is. Do you think they're being fair?'

'I was trailed going to Cap's, knocked off my horse somehow, and put in that old line shack. Then things were made to look like I'd killed the old man. Under those circumstances, what am I to think?'

'That I had a hand in it, of course,' she said.

Ross lifted his eyes to hers, He said, 'I don't really think it, not yet. Not until I get some answers.'

'What are you going to do?'

'Work the place, look for Cap, do what I can. What else?'

'You could sell out and leave.'

'And shout that I was guilty?'

'More than one man has changed his name, gone to Texas or Arizona Territory. Canada isn't far to the north.'

He pushed his plate aside with an angry movement. 'Maybe you even have someone in mind who'll buy the place cheap. Is it easier to get me to sell than it was to get Cap to sell?'

Eden stood up, her hands white on the chair back. 'I had you doped because you were going back to Cap and renege on your bargain. And that wasn't what Cap wanted. Down inside, it wasn't what you wanted. I was only trying to keep you away from him until he had a chance to get out of town. You can believe that or not, as you choose.'

She left then, her anger trembling in the air behind her.

Rube Overman came up and took his seat again. 'Keep your friends, Ross,' he advised. 'A man in your position will need all he can get.'

'What am I supposed to think when—'

'If your thinking goes that way,' Overman interrupted, 'then put your mind on something else.' He watched Ross get up, and added, 'If you want help, we'll do what we can.'

'I'm not sure I want Eden's kind of help,' Ross said.

'I'm not sure,' Rube Overman said dryly, 'that Eden will want to give it much longer.'

Ross turned and walked away.

\*　　　\*　　　\*

Helene Colson stood in the lobby of the hotel and watched Ross coming across the street toward her. Turning, she hurried to the office where Chet Walsh was working.

'Ross is coming here from the saloon. He looks mad.'

Walsh smiled at her. 'I can guess why. How would you feel if you had your drink doped by a "friend" and woke up to find yourself suspected of murder?'

'Ah,' Helene said. 'So it's that way.' She looked down at Walsh. 'From all the talk yesterday and today, Ross is rightly suspected of murdering Cap Mills.'

'There's no proof that Cap's dead,' Walsh pointed out.

'Are you defending Ross?'

He shrugged. 'What business is it of mine?'

'I'm wondering,' she said softly. 'Chet—did you have anything to do with Cap Mills' disappearance?'

'After the agreement we reached?' He looked at her frankly. 'You're the boss. I follow your orders.'

She studied him closely, aware of his smooth charm, feeling herself dangerously close to succumbing to it. She said, 'You decided to come to work for me awfully fast.'

'Only because you requested it Saturday night.' He made a move to push back his chair. 'If you'd rather I didn't, if you can't trust me—'

'Stay where you are,' she said quickly. 'Here comes Ross.'

'That doesn't solve the problem.'

When she opened the door at Ross's rap, her face was calm. She said, 'I've heard, Ross. I'm sorry—about Cap.'

He gave Walsh a surprised glance and

stayed in the doorway. 'Sorry, why?'

'Everyone seems to think he's dead.'

'And so he may be,' Ross said. 'Is there somewhere we can talk, Helene?'

'Here,' she said. 'You know Chet Walsh; he's my new manager.'

'We've met,' Ross said. 'This isn't that kind of business, Helene.'

Chet Walsh swung around, smiling. 'If you mean I should leave—'

'We'll go to my private office,' Helene said. With a hand on Ross's arm, she led the way to the room behind the front office. Her fingertips felt the trembling in Ross and she judged that Chet Walsh had been right. Ross had had a brush with Eden Bruce.

She took Ross's hat and put it on a peg. 'You're in trouble, Ross. If there's anything I can do?'

He studied her, noting the tenderness in her eyes, the compassion in her voice. 'Thanks, Helene. But I'll keep you out of this.'

'Then why did you come?'

'To see you. To find out how you felt.'

She rose and came to stand close to him. 'Should I feel any different toward you because you're accused of this? It's absurd and anyone with any sense knows it.' Looking into his face, she saw the way he was thinking of Eden Bruce. She took a step closer to him. 'A friend proves himself when the going gets difficult, Ross.'

She lifted her hands to his shoulders, and he bent his head to kiss her. The promise she had always held in her kiss was strong today. He could feel it run through her body pressed to his, on her soft mouth, and almost roughly, he drew her against him.

The thin barrier that she had always held against him was no longer there. There was awareness in them only of the other. The distant sounds from the street faded, the muted noises from the rooms above them.

Gently, with a softly trembling laugh, she drew herself away from him and stood back, her breath coming sharply, her cheeks bright with color, her eyes aglow. 'Ross, Ross, this is no time . . .' He could only stand and look at her. She said, 'We have always felt so, Ross. But lately, I haven't been sure. And now . . .'

'And now?' His throat was dry.

'Maybe you're just looking for comfort, Ross.'

Slowly, he went to where his hat hung and lifted it down. At the door, he turned. 'Maybe,' he said. 'Because I can't offer you marriage, Helene. Not until this is cleared up.'

'And then?' She did not dare take a step toward him. The barrier was still down between them.

'And then—if it comes out right. If I find the truth—if I don't hang,' he said, 'I can ask you.'

'As you've asked me before.'

'No,' he said. 'Not as before. I'll not dodge

myself any longer, Helene.' He pulled the door open and strode away.

She stood motionless, listening to his footfalls as he went to the lobby and outside. There was a strong satisfaction in her, a warmth that she could not control. And when she stirred, it was to close and lock the door. She knew herself too well to face Chet Walsh and his charm at a time like this. The barrier still lay crumpled at her feet and she lacked the energy to lift it once more about herself.

Only when the snap of the lock told Walsh what had happened in the room did he move away from the thin partition that separated Helene's room from the office. A woman unsure of herself in love, he thought, was one thing. A woman sure of herself presented another problem. He sat for some time, turning this over in his mind. At last he rose and took his hat and went to dinner. He had made a decision for himself.

## CHAPTER SIX

In more than a week since his recording of the title, Ross felt that he had succeeded in accomplishing almost nothing. He divided his time between working on the ranch and riding in the mountains, following every trail, every idea that came into his mind. At no time was there a trace of anything that might lead him to a solution of Cap Mills' disappearance. There was nothing—no sign—not even a recurrence of the trouble that had plagued the old man.

Cap Mills had disappeared without a trace. It was as if he had really packed up and gone to Seattle.

The last time Ross had visited the sheriff's office, seeking information, the hostility from the town had built up to the point where he could no longer ignore it. Each glance from the silent townspeople was like a blow. And his father had been little more cordial. As a result, he had withdrawn to the cabin, not even seeking the slight comfort he might find with Rube Overman, and deliberately staying away from Helene, thinking that the less he saw of her, the less people would include her in their talk and thoughts.

He was working on the corral fence when the sheriff rode up.

Matt Millard looked sourly at him. 'I've been putting out feelers,' he said. 'No one answering Cap's description has been seen anywhere.'

'I didn't expect it,' Ross said. 'But I expected more to happen here than has.'

'No attacks on you yet?'

'None,' Ross said. 'I suppose now people will say I planned those, too.'

'They're already saying it,' Millard said.

'You put up a good show, running over the mountains hunting. Between that and your friends in town talking you up, some people were almost convinced—for a while. Now they're saying you were behind the attacks in the first place.'

'Thank my friends,' Ross said. 'Rube—and who else?'

'That Bruce girl. You'd think she and not Helene was going to marry you.'

'What about Helene?' Ross asked sharply. 'I want her kept out of this.'

The sheriff shrugged. 'She won't keep. She and that Walsh have been talking you up—pointing out that there's no proof. But that's worn thin, too.'

'And how do they figure I shot at Cap that night, seeing that I was in a jail cell?'

'They're saying you got yourself put there on purpose, and hired the job done.'

'Why didn't I try to fix it so Monk would get the blame?'

'You did—they say. Only I wouldn't listen to you and took Monk to jail, too, and spoiled that part of your plan.'

'Anything else?'

'Yes,' Matt Millard said. 'Some say that Eden Bruce was in it with you. That she doped you all right, but that she pulled you out of it when you two were alone upstairs so you could get rid of Cap.'

'And what does she say to that?'

'Nothing,' the sheriff replied. 'What is there for her to say? She pretends she doesn't hear such talk.'

'So I've been tried and convicted,' Ross murmured. 'Isn't it about time to arrest me?'

'If I had any evidence, I would,' Millard admitted. 'If I don't get any, I'll have to soon anyway.'

'Since when did anyone in Keeler push you into doing anything you didn't want to do?'

Matt Millard looked at his son, a flush on his face. 'I don't like being pushed,' he agreed quietly. 'But what if I resign? They'll elect a new man who'll arrest you fast enough. At least I can give you a little more time.'

'How much time?'

'A week more—that's the limit.'

Ross finished his cigarette while the sheriff rode slowly off, a man solid and bulky in the saddle. Ross knew that even if he wanted to give him more rope, the sheriff could not do so.

'A week,' he said aloud.

\*       \*       \*

Chet Walsh bent over the books, talking to Helene at the next desk without looking at her. 'They won't give young Millard much more time, I'm afraid. There's talk of vigilantes already.'

'I've heard it,' she said quietly.

66

'I wonder,' he murmured, 'if it isn't about time to make him an offer for the place.'

'This is no time to take advantage of him!'

A woman in love, he thought. And a woman sure of herself . . . 'I wasn't thinking of taking advantage,' he said. 'A man on the dodge is better off with cash in his pocket.'

'You think he'll run?' Her voice was scornful.

'It would be better than rotting in a jail cell waiting for a trial that could only result in one verdict,' he pointed out. 'At least it would give him more time—maybe something would turn up if he can wait things out.'

'And meanwhile you develop Cap Mills' land. What kind of reaction would that get?'

'What difference would it make?' Walsh demanded. 'By the time I get things as we want them, I'll have power enough not to care about public reaction.' He added softly, 'And power enough to swing public opinion in the direction I want it—away from Ross Millard. Given time enough.'

Helene was silent. This factor had not occurred to her. Now, studying it, she could see the strength of Walsh's arguments. She said, 'Go ahead and try to buy, then. But what if he won't sell?'

'Then,' he said, 'we'll have to break him out of jail when the time is right.'

'You'd do that—for Ross? Take that risk?'

Chet Walsh turned to look at her for the

first time. 'I work for you. You want him somewhere except on the end of a rope, don't you?'

'I want him alive,' she said. 'And free.'

That night, for the first time in nearly two weeks, Chet Walsh visited the Big Hat. Only this time he went as a guest, not as a dealer. He stopped by the faro table where Eden Bruce was chatting with some customers.

'May I have the pleasure of a dance, Miss Bruce?'

Something in his tone, in the softness of it, warned her. She nodded and stepped away from the table, accompanying him to the floor where they were soon lost in the swirl of dancers, the thump of the music.

He said, 'I think we'd better have a talk as soon as possible.'

'What have we to talk about, Chet?'

He shrugged. 'Ross Millard, sweetheart. But if you're not interested—' He paused and added, 'I've noticed he's cut you lately.'

'All right, Chet.' Her voice was wary.

'Where can we meet?'

'Here,' she said.

'Your decision,' he agreed. 'Say, a bit of supper, when things have quieted?'

Eden nodded mechanically.

The saloon emptied fairly early that night. When only the swamper was left, Eden had her usual supper brought to a table in the far corner. As a rule, she ate this with Rube, but tonight he had retired to his office upstairs, leaving her with Walsh.

She wanted no preliminary sparring. She said, 'What about Ross?'

'One thing, I just thought I'd warn you that Helene Colson is making her position stronger all the time.'

She thought, Am I so obvious in the way I feel about him? She said, 'Why are you telling me this?'

'For two reasons,' he said. 'In the first place, I want to see you get him.'

'Not for my sake,' she said.

He shrugged. 'Partly. Notice that I've settled down as a respectable businessman, Eden. I'm hoping we can let the past stay there—in the past. If you are happy, I'd feel more secure.'

That was logical enough. She said, 'And the other reason?'

'Maybe I'm interested in Miss Colson for myself.'

'Yes,' she admitted. 'You'd have a good deal if you married her.' She looked at him, not hiding her worry. 'That isn't all you have to tell me, Chet,'

'Not all,' he admitted. 'The talk about lynching is gaining strength. Millard is in a bad position. If someone would convince him that he may have to run—it would be safer for him.'

'And—?'

'And prepare a place for him to run to,' he

said flatly.

'And why are you so generous toward Ross, Chet?'

'I told you. What chance do you think I have with Helene as long as he's around?'

'Then you should be interested in seeing him hang.'

'And then comfort the stricken wife-to-be? I'm not that bad, Eden.'

She knew him to be perfectly capable of letting Ross hang, if he thought it would get him Helene or whatever else he wanted. This apparent frankness puzzled her more than she liked to admit.

She said, 'Thanks for the warnings, Chet. Do you have any suggestions?'

He rose. 'Just that you go after the mountain—it isn't coming to you.' With a quick smile, he turned and started away. He hesitated briefly as he saw Ross coming across the dance floor, his step direct and purposeful. He gave Ross a quick nod of greeting and then went quietly out. Had Eden seen his smile, she would have been more disturbed than she was.

Eden Bruce let none of what she felt show on her face as she saw Ross coming. He stopped by the table and said almost roughly, 'What was *he* doing here?'

She thought, He sounds like a jealous husband, and had to suppress a laugh. Whatever hold Helene Colson had on him was evidently not as strong as Walsh thought.

She said, 'Just chatting. Sit down, Ross.'

He dropped into a chair. There was silence and finally she set down her empty coffee cup. 'Well?'

He said abruptly, 'I heard today what they've been saying about you—that you helped me get rid of Cap Mills.'

'I've heard it, too,' she murmured. 'But it means no more than the talk against you, as far as I can see.'

'A woman's reputation and a man's—'

'What reputation do I have?' she demanded with a short laugh. 'It isn't public opinion I worry about.' She went on in a low voice, 'It's your opinion, Ross. You think as you do about my reason for having you doped. And no matter what I say, I condemn myself further before you.'

'I've done a lot of thinking lately,' he said. 'I got to thinking that you'd let them say those things about you and not fight back but just keep on defending me. Maybe I was crazy, even getting the idea in the first place.'

'And you came here to apologize?'

'Perhaps I did,' he admitted. 'And I came to warn you, Eden.'

'Warn me?' She was very still watching him, the strength of his face, the curve of his mouth that was so bitter now.

'The sheriff gave me a week at most,' Ross said. 'If they take me—with this talk, they'll take you, too.'

71

'They might,' she admitted. 'But right now there's more to worry about than the sheriff!' She told him what Walsh had said about lynching. 'There's no process of law to appeal to, Ross. I doubt if they'll wait a week.'

'I come to warn and get warned,' he said.

'What did you expect me to do with your warning?'

'I hadn't thought that far. Run, perhaps. Take the stage for the coast. Sell back to Rube and go East. I don't know.'

'Are you running? Do you plan to?'

'For me to run would be to admit guilt,' he pointed out. Then he saw her face and he nodded. 'And for you as well, now, I suppose.' He looked at her, thinking that somehow he was responsible for the position she had been placed in, knowing it was not necessarily true but feeling no less strongly for all that.

She said quietly, 'On the other hand, Ross, if you run simply to protect yourself from them—the vigilantes or the law—and stay where you can keep fighting, keep looking for Cap, then there might be some sense to it.'

'Hide in the hills, you mean. I've thought of that,' he said, and added, 'but what has that for you?'

'I only ask,' she said, 'so I'll know where to go.'

# CHAPTER SEVEN

What Ross waited for took place the middle of the next morning. He had sent Monk to string fence along the wagon road and was still busying himself with the corral when he heard a rider coming. It was Walsh. Ross straightened from his work and waited to see what was on the man's mind.

'Warming up for summer,' Walsh observed. He took off his black hat and mopped his forehead.

Ross started making a cigarette. 'Seems so.'

Walsh smiled easily. 'But I didn't come to pass the time of day. I came to make you an offer for this place. I hear you've been fixing it up for sale.'

Suspicion rose sharply in Ross and with an effort he curbed it. He said, 'I made no such statement.'

Walsh showed his irritation. 'If you don't plan to sell, say so. If you don't want me around, say that, too.'

Ross realized that he was only defeating himself by being rude. He said, 'Sorry. I'm edgy lately. What's your offer?'

Walsh said slowly, 'Ten thousand cash—for everything.'

It sounded like a large sum of money until Ross stopped to add up what it was buying. He knew horses and he knew the place, and though there was a lot of wasteland to it, the price was ridiculously low.

He shook his head. 'That wouldn't buy much.'

'Then set your price.'

'Buying for yourself?' Ross asked.

Walsh smiled again. 'Any law against it? Any man—even a dealer or bookkeeper or whatever you think me—likes to have something to tie to, Millard. Now, I've always had a hankering for a place in the hills. There's a good view, good water—it would be nice for living.'

He was, Ross thought, too openly wanting the place. Ross said, 'Nice for living, but what about making a living?'

'Cap Mills did. You are. What's your price?'

Ross said slowly, 'Cap's still missing. As long as that goes on, the title is in dispute—in some people's minds. I'm not sure I could sell to anyone legally.'

'I checked that,' Walsh said. 'Legally you can sell, Marsh Whelan says. I'm willing to take the chance.'

Ross nodded. 'Looking at it from Cap's standpoint, I'd say thirty thousand.'

Walsh whistled. 'I hear there's a lot of it wasteland, a lot of poor breeding stock that needs replacing.'

Ross grinned at the change of tune. 'Best water in the hills and good grazing land. It's better for cattle than horses, only Cap was too lazy to run beef.'

'I might go fifteen,' Walsh said carefully.

Ross shook his head. 'See if you can get an authorization on twenty-five thousand.' He saw Walsh's expression and laughed. 'Tell Helene thanks just the same, Walsh. But I don't need that kind of help.'

Walsh was relieved. If Ross had not brought up the subject, he would have had to work around to it. Now he said, 'A man on the dodge could use some cash, Millard. And if you sold it to Helene, you could always get it back when things quieted down.'

'So Helene sent you to warn me—to offer help like this?'

'And any other kind,' Walsh said smoothly. 'The buying offer still stands. Fifteen thousand.'

Ross said, 'I'll let you know.'

Walsh reined his black mare around. 'Don't take too long—you haven't got much time to waste.'

'I know,' Ross murmured, and watched him ride off. Walsh did not go the way he had come, but swung over the trail through the timber that led to the wagon road.

Walsh puzzled him. He could not find it in himself to like the man, despite his apparent efforts to be helpful. It brought Ross's mind around to Helene and he wondered at her motive in this.

His eyes followed the trail where Walsh had disappeared. He turned for the barn. 'I think,' he murmured aloud, 'I'll take a little ride.'

Walsh found Monk where he had seen him earlier that day, stringing fence from tree to tree a short distance back from the road. He drew up and Monk came to meet him, wiping sweat from his heavy face.

'How much longer do I have to do this?' he asked.

'No longer than it takes you to get Millard to fire you. If that's what you want. But Millard will be leaving in a few days-either for jail or on the dodge.'

'That doesn't bring me the money you promised.'

'It's coming,' Walsh said sharply. 'The boys are getting tired of holding the old man, too, but they're smart enough to know it's worth the wait.'

'Why not let a lynch mob go to work?' Monk growled. 'The boys are pretty well lined up. It wouldn't take much to start 'em off. Get rid of Millard once and for all. And the old man.'

'And have the title tied up in litigation for years? No, I want it signed over. I don't care what price tag goes on it.'

Monk said jeeringly, 'And by then Millard will be hid out so they can't find him.'

Walsh laughed at him. 'Hid out all right— but where I put him. Where I can help him.'

He swung the black about and turned down the wagon road for town.

Ross had gone his last hundred yards on foot and he was still twenty yards away when Walsh started for town. He had been unable to hear anything, but Ross doubted if they had been discussing the weather. On the other hand, Walsh could well have been asking questions about the property.

Going back, he got on his roan and came forward to where Monk was loading tools in the wagon. 'Walsh looking for information?' he asked.

'Lots of questions,' Monk said sullenly. 'Seems he wants to buy the place.'

'Seems so,' Ross said. 'Anything special?'

Monk said, 'Nothing special. What the hell's this all about?'

'When a man wants to buy my place, I get curious, that's all.'

'Your place, hell,' Monk said roughly. 'It's Cap Mills' place to me.'

'And me,' Ross agreed mildly. 'That's one reason I'm curious.'

A sudden beat of hoofs came from up the road, followed by the sharp blast of a gun and then a noisy, metallic crash that turned both men in that direction.

\*     \*     \*

Blas Lamesa was not happy; nevertheless he

sang. When he felt too sad about this riding a wagon filled with clinking pots and pans behind a broken-down horse, he would sing a gay Mexican song to cheer himself. When he remembered that he was a *vaquero*, the shame of this he was doing swept over him and he would sing a sad song to tell God and the blessed Virgin that he did not like this and could they not do something for him.

Coming down over the hump of the Keeler range with the noisy wagon clattering behind him, he looked out across the timbered and grassed benches and the great stretch of desert land to the south and he was reminded that he was a cattleman, not a peddler.

But a man must eat, and so Blas Lamesa peered about with his bright, dark eyes, seeking the telltale sign of smoke that would mean a settler's chimney and perhaps the sale of a pot or pan and even, sometimes, a warm meal.

At the foot of the grade, he saw smoke off to his right and a narrow wagon road leading that way. He turned the tired horse into the pathway and jounced along. The timber stopped suddenly, letting the road open onto a broad, grassed clearing. At the far side a good-sized chimney, and just to the right of the building, two men were standing; one of them, a very tall man, carried an axe, the smaller one had a rifle cradled in his arms. Perhaps, Blas Lamesa thought, they are hunting and have found venison for supper.

'*Adelante. Adelante.*'

The man with the rifle was coming toward him, the gun lifted, and shouting something he could not hear for the rattle of the pots and pans. He did not understand this, but when the rifle lifted and sent a bullet that chipped wood from the footboard by his feet, he did.

He swung his horse around and, with the use of a small whip, forced the animal into a run that sent the wagon careening across the meadow. Bullets were flying about him, although he made a poor target. One made a pinging sound as it pierced a pan and the horse leaped forward.

Once Blas Lamesa looked back. The man with the rifle had stopped shooting and was running into the woods, yelling. The older man, the tall one with the axe, had disappeared. A man on horseback, with one arm in a sling, came charging from behind the house and raced his horse toward the woods.

Blas Lamesa followed the wagon road back to the main road and went downgrade along it, not lashing his horse now but letting it have its head.

He soon saw that he had been wise, for when his horse was beginning to stagger, on the verge of exhaustion, he heard the thunder of a rider coming fast from behind. One look and he knew that the trouble was not over. The man with the sling was riding toward him.

Blas Lamesa tried desperately to turn off the road into the timber, but the man reached him and pulled his horse to a halt. Holding the reins awkwardly with his left hand that had the arm in a sling, he shot with the right. Blas felt the wheels of his wagon catch the edge of a rock and then he was thrown in the air. The horse neighed shrilly and fell to its side. The wagon cascaded pots and pans in all directions and came down over Blas. The edge caught him across the arm before he could wriggle completely under it, and then he was in darkness and there were men's voices and the shooting stopped. He heard his horse struggle and finally grow quiet, too weary, he knew, to make an effort to rise.

Ross reined up alongside the wagon and looked at the man with his arm in a sling. He remembered having seen the man hanging around the Big Hat some weeks before. He said, 'Put that gun away, mister.'

From under the wagon, a voice cried, '*Señor, por favor.*'

'What's going on?' Ross demanded.

The rider said, 'There's a Mexican down there. He tried to run me down. I gave it to him. That's all.'

'Sure,' Ross agreed. 'I heard his horse pounding dirt as he came down the slope chasing you.' He disliked this flat, broad face. 'All right, your fun's over.'

'Who you giving orders to?'

Ross reined his roan around, coming alongside the man.

'You, friend,' he said softly. He reached out quickly, catching the man's gun arm. He twisted. The man cried out and the gun fell to the dirt. Ross backed off.

'Now ride,' he said. 'You've had your fun.' He glanced at the wagon. 'You, come on out.'

The man came on hands and knees, inspected the situation carefully, and then stood, one arm dangling limply at his side. He reached over and massaged it, wincing as he did so. He was small and slender, with the sleek dark hair and olive skin of a Mexican.

'What's the trouble?' Ross demanded.

The man shrugged. 'Pots, pans, seesors?'

'What's your name?'

'Blas Lamesa, *señor*.'

Ross said quietly, pointing, 'His gun is there.' He paused. 'If you want to get even with him, go ahead.'

The Mexican jumped for the gun and lifted it. He did not look at the other man, but put the gun in his waistband. Then he smiled. '*Gracias*.'

Ross heard the creaking of a wagon and saw that Monk had the buckboard loaded and was coming toward them.

The man with his arm in a sling said loudly, 'I want my gun back. What kind of a deal you think you're running here?'

Ross, turning, caught the almost

imperceptible shake of the head that Monk gave. Then the man, swearing, turned his horse and cantered back up the slope. Ross watched him.

'Who's that?' he demanded of Monk.

'Logger named Sweeney. Used to hang around the Big Hat until he busted himself up in the woods. I haven't seen him for some time.'

'I hope I see him again when that arm is well,' Ross said.

With a scowl at Blas Lamesa, Monk worked the buckboard about and moved in the direction of town. Ross turned his attention to the Mexican.

'What was this all about?'

Ross had to listen to slow, halting, and very broken English that told him little more than that the man was on his way to the nearest town to sell pots and pans. It took little calculation for Ross to remember he had not seen Sweeney since the night Cap Mills had been shot at—nor that Cap claimed he had winged the man who had shot at him.

He said, 'Let's pick up your stuff and get to town. I'll go along. You just might need an escort.'

# CHAPTER EIGHT

Monk pushed the team as fast as he could to the ranch, unhitched the horses and then saddled his own mount. By following a trail that angled along the creek, he came out on the wagon road some distance above the place where he had left Ross and the Mexican. He pushed the horse faster then, finally turning off toward the meadow along the road Blas Lamesa had come careening down a short while before.

He went across the meadow to the big log building with the smoke coming from the chimney, rode around behind it and went straight to a screen of timber and buckbrush. Monk pushed the horse through the thinnest part of the screen and came out in a deep box canyon backed by the sheer drop of the mountains. A small cabin lay just inside the entrance where a small spring formed almost at the door. A lathered horse was at the tie rail. Monk tied his own horse and walked to the doorway.

It opened to reveal the small, wiry Pickett in the doorway, a rifle in his arms. Monk stepped inside. 'Fine time to start looking to see who's coming. I could have led the U.S. Army in here for all you'd do.'

The rifle went down and Pickett stepped

back. Monk saw Sweeney standing by the stove. 'A big help you were,' Sweeney growled at him. 'Letting Millard run me off that Mexican.'

'You're a damn fool for showing with that arm like it is,' Monk told him. He saw Cap Mills seated on a bunk, his head hanging dispiritedly. 'And I should help you hooraw a Mex peddler.'

'Hooraw, hell,' Sweeney said. 'Pickett had the old man out on the edge of the meadow doing his firewood chore when that Mexican comes in with his wagon and heads straight for Pickett. Pickett got panicky and started shooting. The peddler took off like hell was breathing on him. I figured there was nothing to do but go after him. If he hadn't seen anything, he'd damn well know there was trouble, with Pickett shooting at him that way.'

Monk said sourly, 'And it took you all that time to catch a loaded cart pulled by a spavined horse?'

Sweeney jerked his head at Cap Mills. 'The old fool made a break for it. It took us a spell to calm him down.'

'You hurt him? You know what the boss said . . .'

'Nothing he won't get over,' Pickett answered.

Monk walked over to the old man. 'What'd they do, Cap?' Cap Mills swore at him until he ran out of breath. Monk walked back toward the stove. 'He ain't hurt bad,' he admitted.

'All I did was rope him and run him behind the horse,' Pickett answered. 'He got winded a little.'

'You're crazy. You'll run his heart out doing that,' Monk said. 'And after this, cut your own wood. Leave him alone, you hear?'

'Getting soft, Monk?'

Monk grabbed the little man by the slack of his shirt and shook Pickett until his head wobbled. 'You fool. What do you think the boss is having him kept alive for? I said leave him alone.' He set Pickett down with a jar that made his neck snap.

'All right, all right. But what about that Mexican?'

'He didn't speak good English,' Monk said. 'But, by God,' he glared at Sweeney, 'if he ever gets told what he saw, we're all in for—'

'Get rid of the old man,' Sweeney said quickly. 'Hell, it'll be our word against the Mexican's and—'

Monk reached out and hit him viciously across the mouth. Sweeney fell, cursing.

'Anything happens to him while you're watching, Sweeney, I'll break you in pieces.' Monk swung on Pickett. 'We're riding to town. The boss has got to know about the Mexican. And one of us'll try to catch him before the meeting tonight.' He glared at Sweeney again. 'By then it might be too late.'

\*       \*       \*

Ross took Blas Lamesa to the Big Hat by way of the alley. They left the wagon parked behind the big log building and went in the rear door and up the stairs to Rube Overman's office.

Overman was eating. He looked interestedly at the small man beside Ross.

'You speak Spanish, Rube?'

Overman said, '*Si, señor.*' Blas Lamesa's thin dark face lighted and he loosed a flood of Spanish. Overman held up his hand, laughing. 'Whoa, *amigo*. Those are all the words I know.' The Spanish did not stop and he finally said, '*Todo,*' in a sad voice.

Blas Lamesa looked crestfallen.

Ross said, 'This is serious, Rube. A man named Sweeney was shooting this boy up on the wagon road. Sweeney happens to be wearing his left arm in a sling and—'

'Ah,' Rube said. He rose and walked to a side door and rapped on it. Eden's voice told him to come in. Opening the door, he said, 'Didn't I hear you speak Spanish to a cowboy that was in here from Texas once, Eden? That one that thought we ran a crooked game?'

She was dressed for the street, in a deep pink dress with white at the collar and cuffs. Ross could feel himself stir at the sight of her. 'We had a Mexican housekeeper when I was a girl and—' She broke off as she saw Ross. 'I

86

speak it a little,' she said. 'Not much any more, though.'

Ross explained what had happened. Eden said to Overman, 'Wasn't Sweeney the one who hung around with that scrawny Pickett, working at the hotel doing odd jobs until a few weeks ago?'

Overman nodded. 'Both of them. Then they just disappeared. At least they didn't come in here.'

'When?' Ross demanded.

Overman scratched his jowl and thought back. 'About the time you won the ranch, I'd say. I remember—'

'That was my thought,' Ross said. 'Eden, if you can make head or tail out of what this fellow says, we might get somewhere.'

She turned to Blas and spoke to him haltingly. He listened, nodding, and once asked her to repeat herself. When she stopped, he courteously replied, speaking as slowly as possible, going over his words two or three times before she caught on.

She said to Ross and Overman, 'He was coming down from the Canada Railroad when he saw this smoke and turned in, hoping to sell some pans and maybe get a meal. He saw this tall man and a smaller one in the meadow up near the Hump—I think it's the Hump he's talking about—and when he headed for them the small one started shooting at him. He ran, of course, and a man on horseback came and both he and the man with the rifle went into the timber. Later the one with his arm bandaged came down the trail and shot and—well, you know the rest.'

'Why didn't he fight back?' Ross asked.

Eden said, 'I see you never lived south of this country. He's probably been around long enough to know that—right or wrong—he'd have little chance in a fight. If he won, they'd track him down. If he lost, he'd get short shrift. I imagine he could fight if he had to.'

Blas Lamesa began talking again, and Eden listened carefully. Then she said, 'He says he is a cowboy from Mexico. That he needed money and went to Wyoming on a roundup. The man he worked for got shot and all he had to give him for payment for his work was the cart and horse and pans a peddler had left him. He hopes to be a cowboy again.' She stopped. 'And he's hurt, Rube—look at the way he holds his arm.' Eden went to the boy and began to feel the limp arm. 'Nothing broken,' she said. 'I'll fix that.'

Ross said, 'Whatever he saw, it was up at the old log camp. I've been up there twice lately and found nothing. This time it might be different.' He started for the door.

Eden said, 'Don't be foolish, Ross. You're not going alone—if it is something. And you're not going by daylight.'

'She's right,' Rube Overman said. 'If that was Cap that the boy saw, he'll still be alive tonight.'

Reluctantly, Ross went back and took a seat.

Eden was trying to explain to Blas Lamesa why she was removing his denim jacket. Finally she had it off and his shirt as well. She examined the smooth brown arm, feeling gently but expertly of the muscle and bone. 'Just a bad bruise,' she said.

Ross sat and watched the boy until Eden finished dressing the arm and fashioned a rude sling. She accepted Lamesa's fervent thanks with a smile. Then she glanced over at Ross.

'Tonight is soon enough,' she said. 'Meanwhile, Rube, maybe we had better see what we can find out about this Pickett and Sweeney.'

Rube Overman left the room. When he returned, he nodded to Eden. 'Taken care of. And now?'

'Now,' Ross said, rising, 'I'll tend to some other business.'

Rube looked at Eden and shrugged. There was nothing he could say. Ross's destination was obvious to both of them.

\*     \*     \*

The late afternoon sun was slanting barely over the top of the western ridges as Ross left the Big Hat and crossed the street crowded with Saturday shoppers. None spoke as he

89

threaded his way through them. He had to steel himself against the almost tangible wave of contempt as he entered the hotel.

He saw Chet Walsh at work in the office and rapped on the door. Walsh glanced up and offered his quick smile, beckoning Ross to enter. He did so. Walsh said, 'Come about my offer?'

'I was looking for Helene,' Ross said. 'A man needs time to do a piece of business.'

'So he does.' Walsh hesitated. 'Helene may have gone home, Millard . . .'

There was the sound of a door opening and Helene came from her private office. Ross went to meet her, noting the query in her blue eyes.

He said, 'Let's go where we can talk.'

She led the way into her office, shut the door and stood with her back against it. 'Well, Ross?'

'You mean about Walsh's offer?'

Her lips twisted into a wry smile. 'We weren't very clever, were we? Chet told me that you figured out who was behind it fast enough.'

'No one else in Keeler has that kind of money, Helene.'

'You still haven't answered my question.'

'It's not my place to sell,' he told her. He took a step forward, catching her hands and drawing her toward him. 'That may not be necessary, Helene.'

He was too engrossed in his own hopes to note the expression on her face. 'Not necessary?'

'I mean—I think Cap might be alive.'

'Ross—that's wonderful!'

Laughing, he pulled her into his arms. 'Don't you see, if he is—then this whole thing is over.'

'And our marriage won't have to wait any longer.'

'There's that,' he said. She did not miss the brief hesitation in his voice.

She thought, That Bruce woman is still in his mind. And she withdrew from him, crossing to sit on the edge of a sofa. To Helene Colson, aware of her own attractiveness in contrast to the other woman in the little frontier town, aware, too, of the power that her money gave her, it was inconceivable that Ross could find anything in another woman, particularly a dance-hall hostess.

What had Eden Bruce to offer that she had not? The answer sprang to her mind, sharp and clear. To Helene Colson, there was only one kind of companionship a woman such as Eden Bruce would have to offer.

She rose quickly. 'Ross—if that's true—'

'I'm not sure, of course,' he said. He told her briefly about Blas Lamesa and the incident on the wagon road.

When he was done, she said, 'I think you're right, Ross. But how are you going to get Cap, if there are men like that watching him?'

'At night a man can do a lot of things he couldn't in the daytime.'

'If I can help—'

'Just your encouragement and good wishes,' he said with heavy gallantry.

'I can do more than that,' Helene said. 'Ross, let's celebrate with a supper. At my home. I'll go see about it now. You wait here. I want to talk to you some more.' And before he could answer, she had swirled out of the room.

In the office, Chet Walsh was working industriously at his desk. The fact that he had moved it for 'better light' some time ago had given him a position next to the wall of her private office. Now, though, he only heard her after she came in and called his name twice.

'Eh?' He looked up and then offered her his smile. 'I think the rents this month will be—'

'Hang the rents,' she said. She planted herself before him. 'Is that what you did—kidnap old Cap Mills?'

He should have been prepared for this, after hearing what Ross had said. Knowing that Ross might well hear what was said in here, as he had heard their conversation, he sought a way to quiet Helene's voice. Yet he could not reveal to her that Ross might overhear without exposing his own habit of listening to what went on in her small office.

'I don't understand,' he managed feebly at last.

'Cap Mills,' she said. 'Is that the way you've been doing things, Chet? Trying to hold Cap Mills over my head. And what if we did buy the place from Ross—as long as you have the old man, there's a threat against me, isn't there? A threat to keep me in line?'

He said quietly, soothingly, 'Helene.' He rose, pushing back his chair and trying to move around her to the far side of the room. 'If you feel that way, if you think that is the way I would treat you, my dear, considering my feelings toward you—'

'Go on.'

'—then perhaps we had better dissolve our partnership.'

The flatness of his voice brought her up short. The desire for money, quantities of money, and what it could bring, was Helene's heritage from her father. She was aware that she could carry on their plan without Walsh, but with a great deal more difficulty, and a greater possibility of failure.

She said quickly, 'Then you deny having kidnapped Cap Mills?'

He felt the change in her attitude. He said now, smoothly, 'I don't deny it at all, Helene. But my reason was far different from the one you ascribed to me.'

'Go on,' she said a second time.

Once more, he tried to move around her, away from the wall, separating him from Ross Millard. But, unconsciously, she stood her ground.

'Simply this, my dear. If all else failed with Millard, the very fact that this accusation hangs over him is of some value to us.'

'To let him think—to let me think—that he could hang for killing Cap Mills, when—'

'I apologize for upsetting you,' he murmured. 'But since I had it in my power to clear Millard at any time, I felt no great concern. But you must admit it is a powerful bargaining weapon.'

Helene said, 'A powerful one.' Powerful in more ways than one, she realized. It came into her mind that to lose Ross would be as great a blow as losing this chance at money. If she did not get Ross—by whatever means she could—she would be admitting defeat by a saloon woman. Should Eden Bruce win Ross Millard from her, she saw in it a weakening of her power—and in her imagination she could hear the laughter of Keeler.

Suddenly she smiled at Walsh. 'You're very clever, Chet. Very clever.'

'If we release Mills now,' he pointed out, 'we'll be back where we started, as far as the property is concerned.'

'I know,' she agreed. Walsh had just given her a big advantage over Eden Bruce. That, coupled with her plan for tonight . . .

'Chet,' she said, 'Cap is safe and unhurt?'

'Of course. No one but a fool harms his most valuable assets.'

'Then,' she said, 'maybe if Ross follows this lead and finds it cold—maybe then he'll be easier to deal with.'

'Much easier, I think,' Walsh agreed. He was no longer worried about Ross overhearing. That made no difference in the long run. The work he had been doing when Ross came in had been the delicate business of forging Ross's signature over and over until he had it letter-perfect. He had come across it at the bank while going through some of Helene's business papers and had pocketed it. Once he had the signature sufficiently perfected to place it at the foot of a bill of sale, his problem was solved.

He would simply tell Helene that Ross's wild-goose chase had apparently proved such a disappointment to him that he had gone into hiding. Ross would supposedly contact Walsh, sell for fifteen thousand dollars cash, and then disappear for a short while. Walsh, with the bill of sale to prove his point, would have fifteen thousand dollars and he and Helene would have the property. It would be regrettable that Ross would not return from his 'disappearance' and regrettable that Cap Mills had died in trying to escape his captors. Time and profits, he was sure, would heal what wounds Helene would incur.

But it had depended on Helene ultimately accepting Cap Mills' captivity. He said, 'You'll have to help, Helene. I'll need time to get

Mills out of the way before Ross Millard goes hunting for him.'

She smiled. 'That's well taken care of, Chet.' Turning, she left him alone in the office.

On the chance that Monk had come in early for his Saturday relaxation at the Big Hat, Walsh left the office and went there. He found Monk at a far rear table, playing solitaire with Pickett.

Monk lifted his head as Walsh went by, nodded at the brief signal he received. When Walsh had gone to the bar and ordered a drink, Monk picked up his chips. 'Stay here,' he said to Pickett.

He cashed his chips and left the saloon. He went around the hotel as if he were going to the livery barn and then ducked up the outside rear stairs and eased himself into the upper hallway. He found the door to Walsh's room open and he went in to wait.

Walsh was not long. He came in and began to peel off his coat and shirt. Monk said, 'Millard's got the wind up. Some damn fool Mexican—'

'I heard,' Walsh said. 'I also heard that Millard is riding up there tonight to see if he can find the old man.'

'Ah,' Monk said. 'Ain't it about time we—'

'About time,' Walsh said. 'Leave the old man alone, but I don't care what you do to Millard —just so you get rid of him. Permanently.'

Monk grinned. 'That,' he assured Walsh,

96

'will be a pleasure.' He rose to go and then stopped. 'What if he takes someone else along? The law, maybe?'

'I'll make it my business to see that the law is too involved to go anywhere,' Walsh said. 'It's Saturday night, after all.' He rubbed soap industriously into his face. 'If it should be anyone else, try to get rid of them before Millard reaches the log camp. I want no one but him involved.'

'We'll handle it,' Monk said. He left, whistling softly.

It was a more cheerful sound than Walsh had ever heard the sullen Monk make and for a moment it bothered him. Such deep hatred as Monk Ryker held for Ross could be a dangerous thing. But, he added to himself, at times a useful one.

## CHAPTER NINE

When Helene returned after giving her order for the hotel to fix up one of its rare special suppers and send it to her house, she found Ross reading by the easy chair near the window.

'You took a long time.'

She showed her pleasure at his aggrieved tone. 'Then you missed me. I had some business with the bookkeeper.'

He had heard the mutter of their voices. But it was not in his nature to spy on people and he had deliberately retired to the far side of the room and shut out their voices with his reading.

He took her spring coat from the rack and draped it about her shoulders. She turned her head to smile at him. Her lips were very close, and very lovely.

Ross dipped his head. The violence of his kiss surprised them both. He stepped back, forcing himself to do so. 'Soon there won't be any reason for us to wait, Helene.'

'Soon,' she murmured.

As they left the hotel arm in arm, Ross's eyes strayed over toward the Big Hat. He said suddenly, 'Why can't people keep their tongues to themselves?'

'Does her reputation concern you so much, Ross?'

'That isn't the point,' he answered. 'It's the wrongness of the thing.'

'It could have been anyone who saw you that night. It could have been me they were talking about.'

'I tried to protect you from that,' he said. 'And her.'

She stopped. 'Both of us,' she murmured. 'How important is she, Ross?'

He said, 'You should know better than to ask, Helene.'

It was not enough. Nothing he could say

would ever be enough, she thought, until he said the words she wanted to hear before a minister—and until Eden Bruce was gone. As long as Eden Bruce was about, there would always be doubt in his mind, she thought—and in her own.

*       *       *

They ate in the upstairs sitting room, with a window open to catch the warm breeze from the south. She had ordered cold fowl and then cheese and champagne. It was rare food for Keeler, but Helene's father had been wise enough to stock such things and she had continued the practice. Now she was grateful for his and her own foresight.

Ross would have preferred steak and beer and a slab of pie, but he said nothing except to compliment her on her chef and—later—on her appearance. The wine brought a new sparkle to her eyes and added color to her cheeks. She had never been so gay with him, so free of restraint.

Her gaiety was infectious and he responded to it. After the meal was removed and coffee brought, he relaxed even more, lulled by the warm candlelight and the view of the moon rising over the great stretch of desert. There was an intimacy about their being seated together on the sofa, and a promise of greater intimacy in the way she touched him, in the look in her eyes when she smiled at him.

Finally, Helene murmured, 'That breeze is growing chilly, Ross. If you'd shut the windows . . .'

She went with him to the window and they stood looking through the pane at the spreading moonlight.

'Blow out the candles,' she said.

He did so and returned to her. The wine was warm in his blood, and the fragrance of Helene, so near in the faint light of the moon. He was not surprised when she turned and drew him to her.

The first kiss recalled to him the one recently in her office. It was not Helene who broke away but he. He looked down at her, at the brief strand of moonlight tracing a finger of silver across her blonde hair, heard the quickness of her breathing, the heaviness of his own.

'Ross, Ross,' she murmured. 'There'll be no fancy wedding, no elaborate plans. And it will be soon, my dear.'

His answer was crushed away by her lips, by the pressure of her hands fierce against his back. A thousand melodies in his head, mingled with the perfume of Helene, drowned out the last trace of the thought of what lay ahead for him in the hills that night.

\*　　　\*　　　\*

Sheriff Millard found himself more than usually busy, even for a Saturday night. There was an extraordinary number of fights, of men too drunk to ride home straight in the saddle; there was even one case of a liquored cowboy riding through the town, shooting into the air as few men had dared to do in Keeler for some time. As a result, Matt Millard failed to see the small crew that rode from behind the Big Hat shortly before midnight, heading into the moonlight for the wagon road that led into the hills.

Ross was in the lead, silent, withdrawn. Blas Lamesa and a figure tall and slender in the saddle rode behind him. He had not liked the idea of Eden Bruce going along, but as Rube Overman had pointed out, who else was there for Ross to trust, besides the sheriff? And the sheriff was in no position to go anywhere that night.

The moonlight made the going easy as they followed the wide wagon road toward the foot of the pass that was called the Hump. But once they were near the meadow, the light was brighter than Ross wanted. He stopped and drew Blas and Eden into the shelter of timber.

'This is it,' he said. 'I'll ride in easy and then go on foot. If you hear any ruckus and I don't come out after a while, ride for the sheriff.'

Eden spoke to Blas Lamesa, translating Ross's order. The little Mexican listened carefully, then nodded in his quick way. '*Si, señorita, entiendo.'*

Ross eased his roan quietly toward the meadow. Eden, with equal care, walked her horse up the wagon road toward the upper trail that led into the meadow. Blas stayed where he was, hunched in an old coat of Eden's that was large for him, now and then blowing on his hands to counteract the chill of the mountain air.

She rode with the ease of a veteran, indistinguishable from a man in the heavy shirt and jeans she wore, and when she reached the upper trail, she guided her horse skillfully along the twin ruts of the track. When the timber ended and the meadow began, she pulled her horse to a halt, leaning forward in the saddle to see ahead. But as light as it was, the shadows were deceptive. She moved on, following the rim of trees along the edge of the meadow, seeking to get closer to the black bulk ahead that she knew was the old log camp. Now and then she thought she could make out the form of Ross slipping across the meadow on the other side. But she could not be sure and the silence stretched her nerves.

Blas Lamesa waited the length of time she had ordered, counting to himself until he reached two hundred. Then he turned his horse in the direction Ross had taken and walked it softly over the grassed track.

They were fine people, these gringos. They had helped him when he had neither asked for

102

nor expected help. And now, through the efforts of the *chica*—so *guapa*, too—he was given the opportunity to help them in return. With his left hand sticking from the sling that he felt was totally unnecessary, he guided the horse. With his right he loosened first Sweeney's gun in his holster and then the little knife he carried inside his shirt. There were times when guns made far too much noise.

He barely heard the swish of the rope as he reached the edge of the meadow. The soft sound struck his ears just as he felt the roughness of the hemp against his face, then the rope slipped on down and drew taut.

As he was lifted from the saddle, Blas Lamesa worked his hand free of his shirt where he had been fondling the hilt of his little knife. He held it turned away from him so that when he crashed against the soft, grassy sod it did not turn back and cut him. He lay motionless, fighting for breath, forcing himself to be as quiet as possible.

Footsteps brushed over the grass and a breath heavy with tobacco and whiskey washed across his face. 'Out cold,' a reedy voice said.

Another, which Blas recognized as that of the man with the buckboard Ross had spoken to that day on the trail, said, 'Loop that rope a couple times and leave him. We got work to do.'

Blas waited until the sounds of their going had faded. Then, with catlike ease, he worked the knife against the ropes looped about him and in a moment was free. There was no sound but his own breathing and the movements of his horse tied to a bush a short distance away. He looked out over the meadow but he could see nothing move in the moonlight. Slowly his eyes traveled the edge of the timber, past the heavy black bulk that would be the building head seen by daylight.

Then the sharp, crashing sound of a gun shattered the stillness. Then another, almost directly opposite him. Swiftly, he swung into the saddle and rode straight across the meadow.

Ross kept his horse to the shadow where timber and meadow met until he was almost to the rear end of the wide expanse of grass and then he left the horse, tying it lightly and going forward on foot. He proceeded cautiously but without having to hesitate to get his bearings at any one place. He should be nearly to the upper end where a narrow box canyon opened up behind the old log camp.

His mind turned to Eden Bruce, sitting now in the chill of a mountain night, huddled in a man's clothing, a gun on her hip. Concern for her safety had risen above that of his own problem and had clung there, despite his yielding to Rube's arguments. The dance-hall girl, he thought. The girl that Helene and others had referred to as 'that Bruce woman.' And it came to him that often she stirred him as Helene had done this night, without the magic of wine and moonlight.

'Ah,' he said aloud, and cursed himself. The building loomed close ahead in the darkness. He eased forward, cutting around the corner of the log camp to the screen of timber that blocked off the box canyon.

Once past the screen of timber and beyond an outcropping of rock, he paused. The little cabin set against the slope of the canyon wall could be seen plainly, light glowing from its two windows. There was no sound, no other sign of life about the place.

Ross studied the situation, judging his chances of crossing the twenty yards of open space. Then he crouched like a runner and made a dash through bright moonlight for the cabin corner. He was halfway there when the door swung open. A gun blasted, the bullet kicking up spruce needles at his feet. He hit the ground rolling, reaching for his gun as he did so. The light flung out by the open doorway gave him a glimpse of Sweeney framed there, braced for another shot with the gun held in his good hand.

Ross cursed himself for having stepped into what was obviously a trap. He had his gun out when Sweeney fired again.

Ross managed to fire once, still moving, and Sweeney ducked as the bullet splintered the door frame. He got to his feet, snapping two more shots, driving Sweeney inside. A final sprint carried him to a stand of scrub trees as

Sweeney came out again, shooting.

Then with sharp suddenness the firing stopped. Ross stood where he was, puzzled. Sweeney was just out of his range, waiting as he was, making no effort to continue this fight.

Ross glanced toward the canyon mouth framed by moonlight. A man on horseback stood there, and moonlight glinted on the barrel of his rifle. Before Ross could lift his gun, the man eased back into shadow.

A twig snapped on Ross's left and he swung that way. When he glanced back toward the cabin, the light was gone. In the shadows of the canyon, the darkness was deep and complete. Another twig snapped to Ross's right. Boxed, he thought bitterly.

Then he heard the pounding of hoofs, coming across the grass meadow. Eden, he thought. She and Blas had heard the shots and come running. Not, as he had ordered, gone for the law. He made a sudden dash to his left, knowing that his one chance lay in breaking free.

There was the whisper of someone shifting position ahead of him, the crackle of brush as the man at his rear sprinted forward. He lifted his gun, firing blindly. He had barely time to turn his head at the rising crescendo of noise to his left, knowing it was a rider forcing his way forward on horseback. Then he felt something hard and heavy crash down against his head. He plunged into darkness and lay without moving, his gun arm crumpled beneath him.

## CHAPTER TEN

When she heard the gunshots, Eden spurred toward the long log building that lay half outlined in the sharp moonlight.

She was nearly to it when a single shot came, ahead of her. She swept around the corner of the building and pulled up. There was nothing in front of her but a wall of timber and brush. The sound of a rider came from behind her and she drew her horse to one side, in shadow.

The rider came around the corner of the building. She saw that it was Blas Lamesa, crouched down over the saddle.

'Blas, *aqui!*'

His horse pawed air as he drew the reins in sharply.

'*Señorita?*'

Through the screen of bushes, a rough voice called out, 'Hold it right there, both of you.'

Blas stopped his horse in the shadow alongside Eden. He said to her in his soft voice, 'Go. I will hold them.'

She said, 'I have a gun, too.' She freed it from its holster and leaned forward, calling out, her voice made deep and rough, 'Come out with your hands up. You're surrounded.'

A man laughed. Another voice echoed it. A third jeered. Eden said softly, 'We're the ones who are surrounded.'

'If we could go between the far corner of that building, *señorita*, and the hill, we could be free of them.'

'And leave Ross?'

'Two riding for aid is better than three captured, no?'

'Yes,' she agreed dully. She studied this situation, feeling the silence, knowing the three others had chosen to play a waiting game, a game of nerves, hoping to force their quarry into surrender rather than make a fight of it.

'Go slowly,' she whispered to him. 'I'll talk to them.'

She hear Blas's horse easing deeper into shadow, toward the far corner of the log building. She said loudly, roughly, 'Where is Ross Millard?'

Her answer was the same jeering laughter. Then the deep voice that had spoken before said, 'Ride forward, you two, your hands where we can see 'em.'

'Our hands are on our guns,' she said. 'If we don't see Ross by the time I count ten, we start shooting.' She took a deep breath: 'One ...'

'Two,' a voice mocked from her left.

'Two,' she said. She could feel her throat tighten, ache from the desire to cry. 'Three.'

'Three and a half,' a man piped in a high-pitched voice.

Where was Blas by now? she wondered. Suddenly, a gun broke loose from the near corner of the building. Three shots blended almost as one. A man swore shrilly, with no mockery in his voice now, and then the hard, sharp sound of rifles cracked on the night. She could hear the bullets as they tore wood from the corner of the building, and she could see a burst of flame from the screen of brush and timber directly ahead of her.

She brought up the .38 and fired, once, twice, and then, low in the saddle, she dug spurs into her horse and drove it toward the corner of the building where the hill swept down. Shots sounded, coming from the timber and the other side of the building. She pressed on, flattening herself in the saddle, fighting to keep the panicky horse out of the moonlight.

Then there was the hill and the logs jutting at her. She spurred the horse once more. It went through the narrow space with rock scraping the side of her boot, and she was free. The meadow, bright with moonlight, stretched ahead, and across it, racing for the trees, was a small figure she knew could only be Blas Lamesa. He was on foot and he ran, weaving. Behind him a horseman appeared, the moonlight glinting on the gun in his hand as he brought it up, taking careful aim.

Eden fired. The gun bucked in her hand

and the rider seemed to lift himself from the saddle and disappear. The horse bolted, following Blas.

Eden came alongside the riderless mount, caught the reins, and rode on. Behind her, she could hear the beat of hoofs. Blas had stopped now, looking about, bewildered.

She called, 'Here, quick!'

He broke into a sprint, stumbling over the uneven ground, caught the reins she tossed to him and jumped fluidly into the saddle. They headed for the trees. A bullet whined between them. Another nicked the rump of Eden's horse, nearly sending her out of the saddle as the horse neighed shrilly and leaped sideways. Then the trees lay ahead, deep in shadows, and they plunged into them and pulled up, facing the oncoming riders.

But the two men had stopped and were out of their saddles, bent over the man on the ground. After a moment he rose and stood half supported by one of the men. Blas said, 'He is not dead, that *hombre*. It is too bad.'

'Too bad,' she agreed flatly. 'Your horse?'

'They kill it from beneath me,' he explained. He lifted his gun and appeared to be judging the distance. With a sigh he holstered it. 'Too far,' he said regretfully.

'Should we go back, or try to get to them? With one hurt, we could—'

He broke in, asking her to repeat her words. She did so, and he said, 'It might be wiser to wait, *señorita*. To see what they plan to do, no?'

Eden nodded, suddenly aware of the chill of the night. The men in the meadow had lifted the wounded one to a horse and were riding back the way they had come.

She thought, Surely they don't dare let us go? There was no sound, no sign of life. The meadow lay empty beneath the moonlight. Slowly, the moon dropped, and from behind them the sky paled as the new day worked up from the east.

Finally she said, 'At least we can slip up there and see before it gets too light.'

Blas was off his horse stomping about to keep warm. He blew on his small hands. '*Si*,' he said eagerly.

They rode in the edge of the timber until the hills coming sharply down forced them briefly into the open. There was no challenge, no sign that they had been seen. Puzzled, Eden dismounted and led the horse through the gap between the edge of the building and the hillside. Blas followed and they stood where they had been earlier, looking through the dirty gray morning light at the screen of timber and brush.

'I'm going up there,' she said.

He put a hand out, politely holding her back. 'Permit me, *señorita*.'

She let him go, standing by the horses while he slipped wraithlike into the timber, appearing now and then only as a quick, darting shadow. Then she lost him altogether and she strained to hear his going. But the only sound was that of a raucous jay on a pine limb not far from her. She turned and made a face at it, and when she looked back again, Blas was coming toward her in the open, running

'Nothing,' he said. He spread his hands wide. 'No one at all. A little cabin, but it is empty.'

They mounted and Eden followed Blas to the timber and through the break in the brush. The sight of the box canyon with the cabin near its entrance surprised her. As Blas had said, the cabin was empty. They went around the back, looking for signs of Ross.

Blas found scuffed pine needles and an ejected shell from a gun. That was all. He spent some time in an effort to cut sign and find out where the men had gone. Again he returned with his hands spread wide, empty.

'They didn't come across the meadow,' she said. 'How could they get out of here?'

Blas motioned for her to follow and they rode along the inside of the screen of timber to where it banked against the sharp side of the hill. With some effort, they worked through it and onto a deer trail.

Here and there were signs that might be from riders, but the forest duff was too deep and the light too dim for them to be sure. At last they broke onto the wagon road and any tracks they might have found were lost in the ruts and cut-up surface.

Reluctantly, Eden and Blas rode down the slope and into town.

Weary as she was, Eden went directly to the sheriff's house. He was just waking, sleepy from the long Saturday night, and as he opened the door, he blinked sourly at her.

'It's about Ross,' she said quickly.

'What's he done now?'

'He found Cap Mills—and got shot for his trouble.'

Matt Millard pushed a hand across his face, wiping away the last of the sleep, and stepped aside. She entered, Blas trailing her. The sheriff glanced at him but asked no questions. Eden spoke rapidly, outlining what she knew and what had happened.

'Why didn't you come to me last night?'

'Would you have left town last night on what might have been a wild-goose chase?'

His grunt admitted that she was right. He said, 'I never saw so much trouble in one night.' He swung away from her. 'You say the old logging camp up by the Hump? All right, I'll ride up and take a look. You'll be at the Big Hat if I want you?'

'I'll be there,' she said. She and Blas went away slowly, Eden almost too weary to ride the short distance. She could not help wondering what good the sheriff's trip would be. What use was there in his riding out, now that everything was over?

People would say that it was Ross's way of hiding out, of trying to take suspicion away from himself. And they would say that she had helped him, as she was supposed to have helped him kill Cap Mills. She was the woman from the saloon—without honor, only worthy of being suspect.

She showed Blas to the small room Ross had occupied and then went to her own and fell onto the bed.

## CHAPTER ELEVEN

Chet Walsh was idly dealing himself a hand at a rear table in the Big Hat when he saw Monk Ryker push through the doors and go up to the bar. Monk stood there long enough to have a glass of whiskey and then started for the rear.

He saw Walsh and nodded to him but kept on going. Walsh said, loudly enough to be heard by Rube Overman, seated a few tables away, 'Sit down and have a game, Ryker?'

Monk hesitated, turned, and then sat down casually. 'Make it stud and keep it soft,' he said. 'I ain't too flush right about now.'

Walsh shuffled the deck and tossed Monk's hole card to him. 'Well?' His voice was soft but edged with impatience.

Monk peered at the card and dropped it. 'Ross showed up all right. He left town with that Mexican and someone else I didn't recognize. He placed 'em just off the wagon road and went in alone. One of 'em slipped away, but we dropped a loop on the Mexican before we went after Ross.'

Walsh tossed a three face up before Monk and a nine in front of himself. He leaned back and selected a cigar from his coat pocket. 'That isn't the story I've been hearing.'

Monk grinned. 'I ain't finished yet, Walsh. Ross rode into our trap as neat as you'd want. Only that fool Sweeney tried to shoot him. He was sore about being chased off the Mexican by Ross,' He shrugged. 'Anyway, he ain't hurt except for a sore head.'

'I thought I told you to get rid of him.'

'Why,' Monk murmured, 'what good's a dead Millard to me any more'n a dead Cap Mills is to you?'

He made a small bet and Walsh matched it. He looked at Monk for some time before he said, 'Meaning what?'

'Just what I said. I got a use for Ross, if you haven't.'

Walsh dropped two more cards to the table. 'What about the Mexican and the other one— that was Eden Bruce, by the way.'

Monks heavy face showed surprise. 'A woman? The way she bluffed us and ended by shooting a piece out of Pickett's leg, I'd have thought she was a Texas Ranger. A'mighty, if I'd known . . .'

'You'd what?' Walsh said contemptuously. 'It was a woman, all right. But in a fight, never underestimate her, Monk.'

'You had dealings with the lady before, Walsh?'

'I mean, never underestimate any woman,' Walsh said quickly. 'You haven't finished yet.' He matched Monk's second bet and dealt again. He studied the thick shoulders, the heavy face with the cap of dark hair dropping almost to the eyebrows, the big knotted hands holding the cards, and he wondered if he might not have underestimated Monk.

'The Mexican got loose,' Monk continued. 'We shot his horse from under him and he started running. Pickett went after him and the woman shot Pickett out of the saddle, took his horse and got it to the Mexican. Then they hit for the timber.' He peered at his hole card and upped his bet. He had a pair of fives showing.

Walsh matched him and tossed out the last cards. Monk said, 'We went back and got to Ross and the old man, cleaned the place up, and slipped away without going through the meadow. For all I know, they're still waiting.'

'They came back to town and sent the sheriff up,' Walsh said.

Monk shrugged. 'He won't find nothing.'

'Where'd you take Millard?'

Monk laughed and made a great pretense of

studying his cards. He pushed forward a small bet. Walsh forced himself to concentrate on his hand. He doubled Monk's bet, was called, and flipped up his hole card to show two pair. Monk had three fives and scooped in the pot.

He said, 'You know, Walsh, maybe I'm tired of taking your guff. Now I got the old man and Ross. And one of 'em owns the M-in-C. Think that over.'

Walsh pushed the deck almost gently toward Monk. 'What do you want, a bigger cut?'

'A partnership,' Monk said.

Walsh leaned back and rapped ash from his cigar. 'What else can I do?' He spread his hands in a gesture of resignation. 'It looks like you hold the aces.'

It was too easy, Monk thought. He studied the dealer suspiciously, but saw nothing except poorly hidden and chagrined resignation. It was in Monk's mind that Walsh was an arrogant man, too sure of himself. Monk liked the idea of taking him down a notch, and profiting by it at the same time.

'Nothing you can do,' he said, and guffawed.

Walsh watched him deal. 'Let's get to business, then. What do you plan to do with Millard?'

Monk shook his head. 'Nothing for a while. He'll keep.' He fell silent, playing the hand through before he spoke again. 'What'd the sheriff do about it?'

'He rode back about dinnertime,' Walsh

said. 'He hasn't said anything to me. But the story is all over town.'

Monk pushed his chair back. 'I've had enough.' He glanced down at Walsh. 'How are you going to handle this?'

'I've already started taking care of that,' Walsh said, and Monk swaggered away.

Walsh remained where he was, shuffling the deck in his hand. He didn't like this. As long as Ross was alive, it was too risky to use the bill of sale he had so carefully forged. Should Ross get loose, the whole thing would explode in his face. He dropped the cards, picked up his chips and walked away to cash them in.

Rube Overman was seated at his usual table, his eyes half shut when Walsh walked by. Without looking up, he said, 'Walsh?'

Walsh turned. Overman asked, 'How is Helene taking the news that maybe Ross is cleared of suspicion?'

Walsh smiled. 'If that were the news, she'd take it fine,' he said. 'Only the talk is all the other way again.'

'Oh?' Rube said.

Walsh said, as be had said to a number of others since the sheriff's return to town, 'I hear that there's talk Ross made himself disappear to gain more time and keep away from the law. They say if the story Eden told was true, why wasn't a trace of anyone found. They're the usual bad crop of rumors, but they carry weight no matter how much a man talks against them.'

'The more you point out to a man he's a fool,' Overman said, 'the bigger fool he's going to be.'

'Unfortunately that's true,' Walsh agreed. He started on, then turned again. 'Anyway, I'm talking all I can against such rumors. You might do the same.'

'Why should you?' Overman asked.

Walsh said dryly, 'I think the whole thing is a miscarriage of justice, for one thing. And to be more practical, I have to work for Helene Colson. The happier she is, the easier it is for me.'

'That's honest enough,' Overman said with amusement. He watched Walsh cash his chips and go outside. Then Overman rose and waddled slowly to his office. He paused outside Eden's door and then rapped softly.

Her voice answered immediately and alertly. 'Yes?'

'It's Rube,' he rumbled. 'Busy?'

'Get me some breakfast, will you? I'll be right out.'

When she came into the office, the food was waiting for her. She wore the same clothing she had the night before when she had ridden out with Ross.

'Going somewhere, or just psychic?'

'I didn't think you'd need me on Sunday, Rube.' She paused with her coffee cup lifted. 'Why do you say psychic?'

'Monk Ryker came in and made a great show of looking for nobody and then had a talk with Chet Walsh. I talked with Walsh after Monk left. He's upset about something—I could tell by the way he was so quiet.'

Eden busied herself with eating. 'Go on, Rube.'

'The sheriff found nothing, Eden. I mentioned it to Walsh, and he came back with something about how he thinks Ross was telling the truth, only people were passing rumors that it was a dodge on Ross's part to give himself a chance to hide out.'

'The kind of rumor Chet Walsh would spread.'

Overman looked through his heavy-lidded eyes at her. 'You seem to know a good deal about him.'

Eden pushed back her plate. 'More than I want,' she said. 'So you want to know about it now, Rube?'

'If it will help,' he said.

She told her story briefly, with no emotion. When she was done, Overman nodded. 'That may explain a lot of things. The way I felt, for one. There was nothing wrong in Monk and Walsh having a game, except that Monk said something that made Walsh angry. He hid it fast enough but it kept him upset.'

'And so you waked me—?'

'I just thought you might want to take a little ride tonight—in case Walsh did—and I see I had the right idea. Potsy found some information about Pickett and Sweeney. They drifted in here about three months ago, did odd jobs, then disappeared the same night Cap did. Potsy got the liveryman for a witness, and a couple others.'

'That'll mean nothing,' Eden said.

'Nothing,' Rube Overman said, 'except that the horse Blas rode in on belonged to Pickett. The saddle has his name cut in it. You might want to show that to the sheriff.'

Her smile was radiant. 'Rube! I was so tired, I forgot about that horse and saddle.' She sobered. 'I shot a man last night, Rube. I never thought I could. But it was easy; it—'

'Easy enough when you have a reason,' Rube Overman agreed. 'Don't forget it's easy for others to shoot you, too. The fact that you're a woman won't help much.'

'What do you mean by that?'

Overman poured her another cup from the coffee pot. 'Just that something is shaping up here, Eden. Something I can't put my finger on, but I don't like it. I'd say Walsh is in on it and so is Monk Ryker.' He paused. 'And maybe it's prejudice, but I'll put Helene Colson in there, too.'

'Because Chet went to work for her?'

'It's not that he went to work for her, it's *when* he went to work for her. And he's too busy counteracting rumors about Ross. He's always defending him, first giving the rumor full play and then talking against it. That's an old political trick, Eden. I've seen Walsh's kind before.'

'He's clever,' she said.

'A man like that out-clevers himself sometimes. He gets himself so many wires to pull that one of them gets away from him.' He lit a cigar. 'And I think maybe that happened last night—one wire got away.'

'Do you mean Ross?'

'He's worth something to use for making a bargain.'

She rose. 'Have an eye kept on Chet for me, Rube. I have a few things to do right now.'

Overman watched her go; he hoped he was right. He sensed that under Eden's quiet exterior was an explosive force that could cause her a lot of trouble if she failed to control it.

*       *       *

When Chet Walsh left the saloon, he went to his room, where he washed and dressed. Then he went openly to Helene's mansion, where he had been invited for Sunday dinner.

Helene was alone in the parlor when he was shown in and he could tell by her restless movements that she had been hearing the rumors that had gone around during the day.

She came up to him. 'Chet, what does all this mean?'

'Mean, my dear?'

She waved a hand brusquely. 'There are all sorts of stories going around—that Ross found Cap Mills and has been killed, that he is pretending and is in hiding—oh, everything imaginable.'

'Ross is alive, if that makes you feel better.'

She sat down abruptly. 'Then what did happen? What went wrong?' Walsh did not answer and she stood up, anger blazing in her eyes. 'Chet, just what orders did you give the men?'

'The ones we decided on,' he said. He spent some time looking out the window and then turned to her. 'Helene, I don't like to tell you this but—' He hesitated, waiting.

She went up to him and caught his arm. 'If you have something to say, say it. What happened to Ross?'

Her intensity startled him. Looking down at her, into the angry lines of her face, not quite beautiful now, he wondered if she really could think so much of Ross Millard.

He said, 'I gave the orders, Helene, but some of the boys had their own ideas.' He patted her shoulder. 'I'll figure out something. Meanwhile—'

'What are you talking about?' Her voice was shrill.

'Just that Monk thought he should have a little larger—share, shall we say? He's taken both Cap Mills and Ross and hidden them out

123

somewhere.'

'For what reason? What can he gain?'

'From what he tells me, I gather he wants Ross to sign the place over to him. And Monk is no man to be patient, Helene. He has no intention of letting either of them remain alive once he gets what he wants.' He paused and added, 'Or even if they hesitate too long.'

She was motionless a full minute, staring at him and yet not seeing him. Then she swung about and started for the door, half running.

'Where are you going?'

'To see the sheriff,' she cried at him. 'To get a posse and find Ross. This has gone far enough.'

He blocked her path, catching her roughly. 'Don't be a fool, Helene. Exposing yourself isn't going to help Ross.'

She struggled, crying at him, 'Do you think I can stand by and see him killed after—' She broke off suddenly.

'After .. ?'

'After our decision to clear him,' she said too quickly.

He dropped her arm. He had little trouble understanding her. Her part in last night had been to keep Ross occupied long enough so that his men could move Cap elsewhere. How she had done this was clear to Walsh.

He said, 'Let's sit down and think this out. He's safe enough for a day or so, Helene. If it comes to the worst, you can always get the law.' He escorted her to a chair and seated her. Then he took a brief turn about the room. 'If it hadn't been for that fool Bruce woman,' he said as if to himself.

Helene's head came up. 'What about her?' she demanded sharply.

Walsh saw his advantage and pressed it. 'She rode with Ross last night. When he left here, he went to her and got her help. She and the Mexican. She's the one who came back with the story that Ross had been attacked.'

'I don't understand what you're driving at, Chet.'

He had to do this carefully. Helene was a woman in love, a jealous woman, but she was no fool. He said simply, 'I'm not sure which side she is on.' He had Helene's interest and he went on, 'She's in love with Ross; she told me as much when I worked for her. She'd do almost anything to get him. And a grateful man is often an easy one to manage.'

He paused, and Helene said, 'Go on, Chet.'

'On the other hand,' he said, 'she suspects me, and she would do anything to—hurt me.'

'You?'

He spread his hands. 'You see, my dear, at one time before either of us came here, we were—close friends. There were certain circumstances I shan't go into except to say that Eden Bruce dislikes me intensely.' He smiled at Helene. 'She would suspect me for that, if for no other reason. So I'm not sure

125

just what side she is playing. It could be that she's working with Monk.'

'Against Ross? You said she loved him.'

He did not point out to her that she, herself, was doing much the same thing.

He said, 'Eden's an odd person. I think she's working with Monk in an effort to manipulate Ross into a position where he will need her help. If she succeeds in freeing him, then he will be grateful, you see.'

'I see,' she murmured. 'And if she doesn't succeed?'

'Then I suppose Monk will finish his plan. He hates Ross and he hates Cap Mills. He hates anyone who is successful.'

She was studying him so quietly that he wondered if he had failed. She said, 'Why do you tell me all this, Chet?'

'Why not, Helene? We're partners. It's our mutual concern. Our problem is to get Ross and Cap Mills, isn't it? You must know what we're up against.'

She said scornfully, 'An overly ambitious ranch hand and a saloon girl.'

'Monk is a man who could have been big, given a bit more patience. He's no fool. Eden Bruce comes from a family that owns a good deal of cattle and mining land in Arizona Territory. I met her when she was in a finishing school. She is a person of breeding, yet she knows the ways of horses and cattle and the men who work them.'

It was plain enough. Eden Bruce was a good deal that Helene was not.

Her head lifted, 'What shall we do, Chet?'

This was what he had been waiting for. 'I think I know where Monk has Ross and Cap Mills. Tonight I'll go into the mountains and see if I'm right.'

'And then?'

'Then, my dear, I'll need some help. To take care of Eden Bruce and Monk. That means men—hired men.'

'Ah,' she said, understanding. 'You can have as much money as you need, Chet.' She rose and walked to him, and the intensity of her expression was almost frightening.

'I want Ross alive, Chet. 'What you do to the Bruce woman, I don't care. But I never want to see her here again.'

## CHAPTER TWELVE

Eden Bruce rode alone. The sheriff's reaction to having Pickett's horse and saddle identified for him had not been encouraging. The talk begun by Chet Walsh was taking effect even on Matt Millard. It angered her, and she hoped that when the time came she would have the opportunity of seeing Matt Millard publicly apologize to his son.

When the time came? If the time came, she

amended.

She rode some distance behind Chet Walsh, who was keeping a steady ground-eating pace ahead.

Walsh took the wagon road to the top of the bench and then turned off. Eden saw him one instant outlined against the cloudy night sky and the next the road was empty. At the top of the grade she reined in and sat listening. Finally she made out the faint clop of his horse's hoofs coming from her right.

From her rides through the country, she knew that the trail led to but one place, the M-in-C. From there, a rider could follow a number of routes, down to the desert, into the mountains, back to the wagon road. She sent her horse northward along the road at a fast clip. She was nearly to the northern limits of Cap Mills' land when she swung right, following a trail big enough for a buckboard. The night was dark, with the clouds thickening rapidly over the moon and occasionally she had to slow down, almost feeling her way along the timber-lined trail.

But she figured that she had more open road and less timber trail to travel than Walsh and could reach the M-in-C sooner than he.

She came down on it from above. Where the trails forked, one going to the ranch, the other across the creek and into the mountains, she paused, listening.

From this point the cabin could be seen at

night if there were any lights. But as she looked, it was dark and silent. She heard the sound of hoofs again and drew back into the timber with a calming hand on the neck of her horse.

Walsh went by. He rode low in the saddle, pressing his horse. Eden drew back on the trail and followed.

After a time she thought she knew where they were going. Up near the first widening of the creek was what Cap Mills called his upper meadow, rich summer graze for his horse stock, a round valley cupped in sharp hills so that he needed only to throw a barricade across the narrow lower end to have a natural corral. A solid line shack still stood there along the creek.

She could hear Walsh slowing ahead and soon he went on so softly that she had to strain to catch his sounds at all. Topping a rise, she paused, looking down into the blackness ahead. A moving spot of blackness told her that Walsh was going cautiously up ahead. She heard the faint tinkle of water as he crossed the ford. And then the dark patch separated, and she realized he was on foot, leading his horse.

She did the same, dismounting after she crossed the creek. She would have walked into Walsh's horse, tethered just off the trail, had not her own mount sensed the other and thrown back its head in a sudden move. She turned quickly and clamped a hand over its nostrils. When it was calmer, she led it back a way and tied it off the trail and once more went forward on foot.

She stopped as she reached the opening to the meadow. She could hear Walsh ahead and then, suddenly, a voice came sharply from the darkness.

'Hold it right there.'

She drew her gun, not liking the feel of it in her hand, remembering the night before and knowing that she would do the same again if there was need.

\* \* \*

When Walsh heard the challenge, he said softly, 'Sweeney, keep your voice down. This is Walsh.' He struck a match, cupping it to his face. Sweeney's answer was a grunt and the sound of a gun cocking. Walsh moved forward softly, his gun along his leg.

'Where is Monk?'

'Around.'

'Where is Millard?'

Sweeney's voice was mocking. 'Didn't Monk tell you?'

'No,' Walsh said with dangerous softness, 'but you're going to tell me.' He stepped forward, one hand driving Sweeney's gun into the air, his other driving his own gun into Sweeney's ribs. 'Drop your gun and turn

130

around.'

Sweeney did as he was told. Walsh could hear his heavy breathing and he knew that the man was afraid. 'Who is in the cabin?'

'The old man.'

'Where is Millard?'

'You go to hell, Walsh. Me and Monk figured we got more coming than lousy wages—the work we're doing.'

'And Pickett?'

'Figure that out for yourself,' Sweeney said.

'What do you gain by crossing me?' Walsh demanded. 'Do you and Monk think you can run this as well as I?' His voice lashed at Sweeney scornfully. 'You're a fool, Sweeney.'

'Could be, but I'm sticking with Monk.' His voice taunted Walsh. 'We got it pretty well figured out.'

'What to do with Millard and Mills?'

'Yep,' Sweeney said.

'And what to do with—this?' The roll of the gunshot swelled over the meadow and then faded to a whisper. Walsh stood, his eyes on Sweeney, watching him take a step forward and then fall to the ground, his arms outstretched.

Slowly Walsh holstered his gun. Then he turned and went to where Sweeney's gun had dropped. Picking it up, he held his hat in one hand and aimed the gun with the other. The closeness of the bullet to his hand as it went through the crown of the hat startled him. He laughed a little to himself.

There was a single lamp burning, casting dim light through one dirt-encrusted window. He left his horse next to Sweeney's at the rail and walked quickly to the house. He pushed open the door with one hand, Sweeney's gun ready in the other. Sweeney had told the truth. There was no one there but Cap Mills.

The old man sat on his bunk at the rear, a heavy chain around one leg, the other end locked to a spike in the wall.

Walsh said, 'Thank God!' He crossed the room and from pleasure his expression changed to indignation. 'They have you chained like an animal!'

The wary lines of Cap Mills' face were set with suspicion. 'What's your game?'

Walsh laid the gun casually on the bunk by Cap and then bent to the chain. 'Game? Is that any way to talk to a friend?'

'What brought you here?'

Walsh said smoothly, 'I'm Walsh; I used to be dealer at the Big Hat. I was dealing today, just for fun and—well, a dealer hears lots of things. A fellow named Ryker—Monk Ryker—'

'Know him. He worked for me.'

Walsh nodded. 'He was talking to a little runt by the name of Pickett, I think. I heard enough to have a hunch you might be here. So I came.'

'I heard some shooting.'

'There was a guard,' Walsh said. He lifted a

132

hand to his hat. 'He shot and missed. I didn't.'

Cap grunted. 'What's your stake in this?' He moved his hand slowly toward the gun on the bunk.

Walsh stood up. 'I wonder if there's a key for this lock on that man out in the meadow.'

'Yep,' Cap said. 'But that don't answer my question.'

Walsh shook his head. 'You're feisty considering the position you're in.'

'I thank you,' the old man said with grave courtesy. 'And I'll thank you more when the chain is off.' He scowled down at it. 'I was working on it myself. But doing this don't answer my question.'

Walsh chuckled. 'So it doesn't. I'm looking for Ross Millard. I was surprised to find you alive.'

'That crew caught Ross today,' the old man said. 'I heard it.' He swore with the accumulated vocabulary of close to seventy years.

'Monk's planning to kill him,' Walsh said. 'I heard him plan to kill you and Ross both and make it look like a gun fight.'

'Heard them talking,' the old man said. 'Either that or he was going to kill me and let the sheriff discover it and accuse Ross.' He snorted. 'Matt Millard is fool enough to swallow that, too.'

Walsh said eagerly, almost too eagerly, 'Where did they take Ross?'

'I wish I knew,' Cap Mills said.

Walsh left the cabin, and in a few minutes was back with a key. Shortly Cap was free of the chain.

'Where could he have taken Ross?' Walsh demanded.

The old man picked up the gun and thrust it into the waistband of his trousers. 'I could guess mighty close.'

'If you're feeling fit to ride then,' Walsh said, 'let's go.'

Cap took Sweeney's horse. Halfway across the meadow he spoke again. 'What you so set on helping Ross for?'

'Because I think he got a raw deal and—' Walsh paused and laughed. 'I'll be frank, Mills. I've been trying to buy the M-in-C from him.' He added, 'I thought he owned it.'

'He does,' Cap Mills said. 'I signed it over fair and square.'

They rode in silence to the road. The old man turned down toward town. He said, 'Did Ross agree to sell to you?'

'He said he'd let me know next week sometime.'

'Might as well sell if he's on his way to hanging,' the old man said.

They worked on beyond the meadow to a small tightly fenced meadow. 'There's a line shack up here where I keep some breeding stock,' Mills said. 'I figure it's a good place.'

'Go easy,' Walsh said. 'Monk might be—'

'Don't teach an old hound like me to steal chickens,' the old man retorted. He reined in his horse and slipped out of the saddle. Walsh followed suit and they moved forward on foot. Before long he made out a timber-ringed clearing, fenced, and just ahead of them, a small shack. Light spilled out the one window onto the ground. A saddled horse was standing before the door.

'Monk,' Walsh whispered.

'Could be. Don't recognize the horse from here.' Cap moved forward, as quiet and sure-footed as an Indian. Walsh found himself hard put to keep a pace behind.

A half-dozen steps from the corner of the house, the old man stopped beside a low-branched spruce. 'Now,' he said, 'before we go any farther, I'm obliged to know what you figure on doing.'

'Doing? Get Ross.'

'Yep,' the old man said 'Then you'll have both of us. Think I didn't spot you the minute you walked in?' His voice changed to soft mimicry. 'Over here, Mills . . . We'll take care of him. You do the rest here. And see that you make it look good.'

Walsh started forward, reaching for his gun.

Cap said, 'Mine is out and pointed at your belly, friend. Just rein up.' He shifted his position slightly. 'You'll walk ahead. Now that you and Monk have crossed each other, it'll be interesting to see what happens when you get

135

into sight. Move, mister!'

Walsh started forward. A single shot boomed from inside the cabin, sharply.

## CHAPTER THIRTEEN

When Ross climbed back from the deep blackness he had lain in, he could only sit while he waited for the throbbing at the base of his skull to stop. It took a few minutes for him to recognize the tiny cabin he was in, the one where Cap had always summered his best breeding stock.

He made an effort to lift his hands to his face and then he discovered that they were tied. He strained against the ropes, throwing himself sideways and gasping as the rope, cleverly knotted about his waist, cut against his wind.

He lay for a moment, gathering his strength. Thin sunlight was coming in through the one dirt-smeared windowpane, and by its angle he could tell that it was turning toward afternoon. The air was thin and cold here and he could feel the chill of the room bite into him.

Thinking back, he realized that he had been unconscious nearly twelve hours. He grimaced. It was a real blow he had taken.

He was tied into the bunk, in a half-slumped position, the rope about his waist not preventing him from lying back but keeping him from sitting quite upright. He could feel the bite of rope about his ankles and wrists. Whoever had tied him had done a workmanlike job of it.

He lay back down, shutting his eyes to lessen the pain in his head. He fell asleep and when he awakened again the room was dim with the oncoming night. Someone was at the front by the stove. He could smell coffee and frying bacon. He made an effort to sit up and found that the sleep had put a good deal of strength back into him, as well as giving him an appetite.

He leaned forward and saw Monk Ryker standing by the stove, dishing steaming beans into a tin plate. Monk glanced his way and gave him a crooked grin.

'Too bad. I thought you was dead.'

'Let me out of this and we'll see who's dead.'

'That,' Monk answered, 'wouldn't be smart, now, would it?'

Ross grunted and lay back. It was a surprise to find Monk here; he could not understand it.

When Monk had the food dished, he brought it over, beans and bacon, and a slab of bread, and coffee in a tin cup. He set them down on a broken-backed chair, moved the other chair and the rickety table into a position that gave him a straight-on view of Ross, and put his own food on it. His gun in one hand, he eased the ropes about Ross's wrists so that with a little effort he could work free of them. Then Monk sat down to eat, the gun beside his plate.

'What's your stake in this?' Ross demanded.

'Eat your supper,' Monk said.

Ross rubbed his wrists until the feeling came back to them and then reached for his food. He ate avidly, too hungry to care that the scalding coffee scorched his mouth.

When the edge of his hunger was gone, he looked up from his plate. Monk was through, sitting and watching him with a cigarette hanging from his lips.

'What's your stake in this?' Ross asked again.

'I crave to be a man of property like you, maybe. The M-in-C would be a nice place to start on.'

'Ah,' Ross murmured. 'Then you're the one who was pushing Cap.' Monk made no answer. 'Do you think holding me will get you anything?'

'Might get me a bill of sale for the M-in-C,' Monk told him.

'In exchange for what?'

'A horse, some grub, and an escort over the Hump to the Canada Railroad,' Monk said. His eyes flicked across Ross.

Ross laughed at him. 'I was wrong. You weren't the one pushing Cap, Monk. You were just hired for it. You aren't smart enough to have done it on your own.'

Monk swore at him. Ross stretched, feeling the strength flow back into him as the food took hold. He drained his coffee cup and leaned back, rolling a cigarette. Ross was under no illusions about Monk. The man had always hated him with a deep, burning hatred. Occasionally they had fought, but Monk had never found any way to quench that flame inside him. Now, Ross thought, he had his chance. Ross's payment for a bill of sale would be a bullet, not a ride to the Canada Railroad.

'Who's behind you, Monk?'

Monk's answer was a shrug. Rising, he took his gun and approached Ross. Ross took a final drag on his cigarette, tossed it into his coffee cup and let himself be tied.

He said, 'That gun's too real. You'd like too well to use it, Monk.'

Monk worked with one hand, twisting the rope about Ross's tensed wrists quickly, making a hard, fast knot. When he had finished, Ross stretched out on the bunk. Monk turned away with a grunt and got himself some more coffee.

Ross lay where he was, dozing now and then, working to bring his strength back fully. The rope on his wrists was slightly loose whenever he relaxed his muscles, taut when he tensed them as he had on being tied. When Monk was not looking, he tried to gain room in them but he realized it would take more than a moment to free himself.

Finally he rolled over, his back to Monk. 'Blow out that damned light and let a man sleep,' he said.

Monk raised the wick a little higher. Ross stayed where he was, his breathing slowly becoming soft and steady. Now and then he would twitch, as a man dreaming, but most of the time he lay still, the part of his back that was visible to Monk rising and falling in steady rhythm.

It was nearly midnight, he judged. He wondered if the man intended to go to bed. He rolled over, keeping his wrists hidden so that Monk wouldn't see the slackness of the rope about them. Monk was upright in his chair, his head dropped to one side. He woke with a start as the rawhide springs beneath Ross creaked.

Ross said, 'Better stay awake, Monk. I might run out on you.'

'To hell with it,' Monk said. 'I'm going to bed.'

'Waiting for someone?'

Monk walked across the room and reached to pull himself to the upper bunk. He held his gun carefully in his left hand. He was halfway up, one leg on the edge of Ross's bunk, the other knee cocked over the upper, when Ross slipped the ropes and moved.

His hand lashed out, catching Monk by the calf of the leg. With a wrench that sent the rope cutting cruelly into his midriff, Ross jerked. When Monk slammed to the floor on his back, Ross still had a grip on one heavy ankle.

The breath went out of Monk in a rush. He twisted, gasping for air, lifting his gun blindly. He fired and Ross felt the searing heat of a bullet along his side. He jerked again, twisting Monk so that his heavy torso fought against his hip socket. Monk screamed.

Outside, a man's voice shouted. Ross thought, Whoever he was waiting for is coming in. He freed one hand from Monk's leg and, grasping his pillow, threw it at the lamp. The pillow struck and carried the lamp over with it. A jet of flame leaped out, caught spilled oil, and then ate hungrily into the tinder-dry floor boards.

He renewed his grip an Monk's leg as a kick nearly tore it loose from him. He wrenched again, and once more Monk screamed with pain. Monk was on his face now, his leg cruelly twisted, and he clawed at the floor for purchase. Ross pulled, fighting with every ounce of strength he possessed to drag the heavy body toward him.

Monk threw himself violently over on his back, seeking to lift the gun still clasped in his left hand. Ross saw the move and threw his weight against Monk's leg in the direction opposite from which Monk's body was going.

There was a bubbling shriek. Monk lifted

his other foot as high as he could. Ross felt the heel of it strike his arm. For a moment he thought the bone was shattered and the sheer pain of it made him loosen his grip and sag backward. Then he fought himself forward, reaching again for Monk. He found only air.

He looked down and saw Monk on his face on the floor, motionless. He rubbed at his arm and felt life coming back into it. Quickly, he ripped at the cords around his feet and his waist. In a moment he stood, staggering on his numb feet, catching the edge of the upper bunk and hanging onto it until he was able to handle himself. He glanced toward the fire and saw that it was reaching the wall now, still small but fingering out in every direction.

Ross bent and got Monk's gun, thrusting it into his own holster. He jerked Monk upright, drove his shoulder beneath Monk's belly and lifted. Monk dangling, he staggered toward the doorway. Whoever was outside had made no sound for some time and he could only take the chance and go up against them.

A muffled voice cried, 'Watch . . .' There was the flame of a gun. Ross threw Monk aside as he heard the sound of a bullet striking flesh, and he leaped for the cover of darkness at the corner of the cabin, clawing at his holster.

There was the noise of someone running, a man shouting. A gun rapped out again. Ross went in the direction of the firing, toward the cover of timber near the cabin. He heard his name called and then he struck something with his knees. He went forward, lit on his shoulder, rolled and came to his feet. Again the gun sounded. He ran for the sound, stumbled over a root, cursed, rose and ran on.

Whoever was ahead had found a horse and was making tracks. Ross swung around, saw Monk's horse rearing against its reins as the firelight leaped against the window almost in its face. There was the beat of three horses ahead now, and Ross ripped the rein free and thrust a foot toward the stirrup. Light flamed through the window, showing him Monk's body lying sprawled just before the door. He turned and ran to the man, rolling him over and feeling for a heartbeat.

It was there, solid and steady. A quick motion with his hands told Ross that Monk's wound was in the thick part of his leg. He dragged Monk clear of the cabin, swung into the saddle, and headed the horse toward the upper meadow. The sounds of the three riders were fainter now, and he forced Monk's solid, close-coupled animal to more speed.

The pain of the bullet burn along his side was beginning to work up in him. His head throbbed and with the weakness came a numbness in the arm Monk had kicked. He fought the horse to hold it on the steep downgrade dropping into the meadow. It seemed once that all sounds of running horses had faded, and then he heard them again and knew he had fainted momentarily. Once he thought the ground was rushing up to strike his face and he came to, clinging to the horn. The third time he slumped forward and stayed that way, unaware that the horse raced on, heading for the only place it felt secure, the barn at the M-in-C.

*       *       *

Ross felt the shock of cold water on his face and the taste of it on his parched lips. He opened his eyes and saw the moonlike features of Rube Overman and shut his eyes again. Then the splash of water was sharp and drenching, and he sat up with a gasp. Rube Overman held a dripping bucket in his band.

'Where's Eden?' he demanded in his soft voice.

Ross shook his head and winced. 'Eden?' he repeated.

Rube Overman emptied the bucket over Ross's head and tossed it aside. Ross got to his feet, brushing the water away, his mind clearing rapidly now. In the east the first hint of the sun was appearing and around him the M-in-C lay quietly in the gray dawn light.

'What about Eden?' Ross demanded.

Rube Overman took him by the arm and steered him toward his buggy close by. 'She rode out last night, alone,' he said. 'She didn't show up and I woke early. She wasn't in her room and so I started up here. I got about a half mile beyond here when you came riding hell-bent, out cold on Monk Ryker's horse. He stopped here, fortunately. You were about out of the saddle.'

'Monk's in the hills, shot,' Ross told him. He recounted what had happened. 'But if Eden was there—'

'Eden was there and so was Walsh,' Overman said. 'It was Walsh she went after, at any rate.' He lifted the reins and started the buggy into motion. 'Maybe she hit for town along the other road.'

'If it was Eden there,' Ross said, 'why didn't she identify herself?'

'Did you, when your name was called? In that darkness?' Overman snorted. 'My guess is that she heard horses going off, like you did, and took out, figuring it was you.'

Ross said, 'Where is she, then? I was following them when I went out.'

Rube Overman said, forcing the buggy horse to a faster pace, 'From what you told me, I'd say it's a job for the sheriff.'


## CHAPTER FOURTEEN

Ross said, 'This is foolishness. Can't those fools out there see that I'm telling the truth?'

His father watched the doctor, who was

working on Ross's wounded side. He said, 'Whether they're fools or not is a matter of opinion, son.' He listened to the restless movements of the mob gathering in front of the jail. 'They're stirred up.'

'Why?' Ross demanded. He winced as the doctor poured something hot on the bullet burn. 'Do they think I'd shoot myself and then knock myself out?'

'Right now,' his father said, 'they're thinking what they're told to think. And Monk Ryker is doing the telling.' He looked through the barred window of the cell where Ross lay. A pair of guards were stationed within view, solid, respectable townsmen, pacing up and down, carrying rifles, the stubborn conviction of their rightness reflected on their faces.

'I can't think for them,' he said. 'And Monk did a convincing job. After all, he's got a leg shot up, too.'

'I told you it was Walsh that did that,' Ross said.

The doctor finished wrapping the bandage on him and straightened up.

'Take it easy,' he said. 'If you get a chance.' He looked at the sheriff. 'I'd better go home and prepare for the rush. It sounds like hell will break loose around here before long.'

'It will,' Matt Millard said with soft savagery. 'I'll let no mob take any prisoner of mine.'

He went out with the doctor and Ross lay

146

on the bunk, listening to the growing mob, unable to comprehend this, and yet realizing that it could not be denied. Slowly he pieced it together, step by step, from the day he had been given a lame horse by Monk and had come charging back to town, looking for a fight to vent his anger.

He thought now, I walked right into their trap.

Monk and Walsh working together. He was sure of that now, even if he only had Overman's shrewd guess for proof. Monk and Walsh with Pickett and Sweeney maneuvering him into a trap—with a lot of help from himself—and Walsh cleverly working on the town to get it in the mood for this that was outside now.

His father came back with coffee. He handed Ross a cup and then sat on the edge of the bunk across the small cell. 'They're getting worked up,' he said. 'It's coming, no matter what I do.' He looked old and tired. For the first time since he could remember, Ross felt a surge of sympathy for this man.

He said quietly, 'I've told you the whole thing. I don't know what their game is, but that's the way it sets now.'

Sheriff Millard blew on his coffee and looked at his son. 'It's not my place to say you're telling the truth or lying. That's for the court to decide. But it *is* my place to protect you until a court can make its decision.'

147

'If I could talk to them,' Ross said.

His father's laugh was short, abrupt. 'After what Monk has told them? That he caught you trying to slip Cap Mills farther into the hills—you and that Mexican confederate of yours you've had around, hidden? After Monk saying that you shot him and left him in that cabin and set it afire?'

'What about Walsh?' Ross demanded.

'What proof is there except Overman's hunch?' the sheriff demanded logically. 'See it from their point of view, Ross. They've been convinced for a long time you were behind all this. Now they're saying I'm protecting you because you're my son, not because you're innocent. My word has lost its weight around here.'

'Walsh and Eden Bruce,' Ross said stubbornly. 'And Rube can prove that Blas Lamesa has been in the saloon all the time. Doesn't Rube's word have any meaning?'

'Not much,' Millard said. 'Because Lamesa disappeared last night. He rode out on that horse of Sweeney's.'

Ross could understand this. The little Mexican's face had been understandable even if his language had not. He was grateful both to Ross and Eden for the little they had done for him, and he would repay them. Ross was sure he had gone after Eden in an effort to protect her. But what good was this knowledge?

'Eden Bruce,' his father said, 'is put on both sides of the picture, depending on who's doing the telling. Right now most of 'em think she's in with you. Her being gone doesn't help you, boy.'

Ross was aware of the stiff look on his father's rugged features, and he said, 'Go on—you haven't said it all.'

Matt Millard gulped at his coffee and set the cup aside. 'Just this. The law isn't idle, son. I've had feelers out—on this Walsh, on the girl, on any new one who comes in here and settles. That's saved this town trouble before and it will again.'

He hesitated once more and Ross said, 'Go on.'

'Walsh is a gambler. He's got his name in a half-dozen sheriff's books from Arizona Territory to Oregon. There's an extradite order out for him in Missouri, too.' He lifted his coffee cup and set it down with a sigh. 'Eden Bruce was with him for two years or so—then she disappeared for a couple more. She turned up here.'

Ross said through a dry throat, 'His wife?'

'Supposed to be. His woman, anyway. When she was eighteen she ran away from a finishing school, East. She comes from an Arizona family, a fancy one. That's not news, that's public, Ross. Her family has power enough to keep a lot of things quiet.'

Ross felt the sickness rise in him. Eden and

149

Chet Walsh—and the way he had been hindered last night so that Walsh had time to ride free. The three horses pounding down the road. Eden and Walsh chasing Cap Mills, maybe. The bitterness in him at the realization that his first hunch had been right was strong and violent.

He said, 'I want to talk to Rube, Sheriff.'

His father rose and walked out. Ross sat on the bunk, drinking his coffee and smoking, shutting out everything from his mind.

Rube Overman waddled in at dusk, with Potsy, the floor man, carrying a tray of food. Ross had no appetite but he was grateful. Potsy set the tray down, his long face lugubrious.

Rube said, 'Potsy tells me Helene Colson has a hired crew around her. I think maybe you'll get out of here soon.'

'Keep Helene out of it,' Ross said.

Rube studied him, his shrewd mind turning this over and seeing what was eating Ross. He said, 'Go chin with the sheriff, Potsy.'

Potsy drifted out and Overman sat down on the opposite bunk with a sigh. 'You eat that supper, Ross. You need all the strength you can get.'

Ross turned to the tray. Rube went on, 'It's Eden, isn't it?'

'I heard,' Ross said briefly, 'about her and Walsh.'

'I've known it for a while,' Rube Overman

said. 'It makes no difference except to make me admire her a mite more. And there's a lot to admire in that girl.'

Ross was bitter. 'To admire someone that pretends one thing and does another, who cuts your throat while stroking your hair?'

Overman nodded. 'There you're wrong. She hid nothing except to protect herself. What she knew about Chet Walsh was only valuable as long as it wasn't generally known. It was something to keep him in line. She's all woman, boy. What was done, she figured her fault as much as his. She left as soon as she was old enough to see the truth about the man. Are you censuring her for being young?'

Ross winced. His own youth was nothing to point back to with pride. He said, 'You make me doubt myself, Rube. But what about the things she's done? Knocking me out with that drink the night Cap disappeared? Going up with me to the meadow, where she rode off free and I ended up Monk's prisoner. Getting in my way last night so Walsh could ride free?'

'Now you're thinking like that mob out there. You're seeing it all one way—and it could be more than one.'

'So it could,' Ross agreed. 'It changes nothing, even so, Rube. I can't do anything locked up in here. I was a fool to agree to go to jail in the first place.'

'This morning,' Rube said dryly, 'you were hardly in a position to argue. You didn't have

151

the strength to kick a baby.'

He got up and took the empty tray, 'There'll come a chance. You just be ready for it.' He paused at the cell door and rapped a spoon across it, asking for release. 'And think both ways about Eden, Ross. All people make mistakes; few of them have the umption to try and square the ones they've made. And fewer still can admit they've made them.'

Sheriff Millard came and unlocked the door, and Rule waddled out, The door clanged shut, the key turned, and the sheriff followed Overman.

Ross lay still, the darkness thickening, wondering when Monk would have this mob stirred up enough to defy the law and attack.

He turned over in his mind what Rube Overman had said. He forced himself to withhold judgment, to wait until he saw Eden and Chet Walsh, to see and hear for himself.

The darkness grew deeper until the light from outside was only a small square of pale black, visible by contrast with the heavier darkness of the cell. Ross sat up, testing his side and finding that the pain of movement was lessened, that he had mostly stiffness left. He walked about in easy, steady strides.

Once he stopped, hearing a noise outside the cell window. But it was not repeated and so he kept on walking. The mob sound from beyond was a low restlessness like wind in the timber.

He heard the noise outside the window again and once more he stopped. A boot on hard dirt, he thought. The sound of something striking the log wall of the building. He eased forward, flattening himself against the wall.

'Ross?'

It was Helene Colson and the shock held him mute for a moment. Then he said, 'Be careful. There're guards in the alley.'

'Not any more,' she said. 'Ross, I have men out here.'

'Keep out of this, Helene,' he said sharply. 'Those men in front are ugly. They'll—'

'And leave you to them?' she interrupted softly. 'Ross—'

He went to the window and reached out to touch her hands holding to the bars there. The faint light of the moon through thick clouds was enough for him to see the beauty of her. She was dressed for riding, though he knew she had little skill on a horse. She wore the Eastern garb of tight pants and a shirtwaist, and despite the pressure on him, the sight of her figure molded by the clothing stirred him.

'Keep out of it,' he said again, but more softly.

Helene said, 'The talk is that my bookkeeper, Walsh, and that Bruce girl are involved, Ross.'

'So they might be.' Looking at her, thinking that she had brought a crew of men to help him, an idea took hold and formed quickly.

'Helene, there is something you can do . . .'

'Anything, Ross.' Her voice was husky.

'I think Walsh has Cap Mills.' He sketched the events of the night before swiftly. 'I don't know where Eden stands, but—'

'I think I do,' she interrupted.

'Listen,' he said. 'My guess is they'll have gone back to the logging camp. That box canyon in there can be held against an army. If they haven't gone over the Hump to the railroad, that's where they'll be. If you'll send your men there—'

'And you?'

'I'll be along,' he said. 'You go home and wait, Helene. Keep the coffee pot on the stove.'

'The wife waiting for the husband to come home from the wars?' Helene said.

'Ah,' Ross murmured. 'So it could be.'

Their hands touched and she stepped back out of sight. He stood by the cell window, listening to the sounds as she and her men moved away. He wondered how long it would be before the disappearance of the guards was noted—and he knew that if he acted at all, it would have to be before then.

# CHAPTER FIFTEEN

When Rube left Ross, walking behind Potsy, who carried the food tray, he went slowly through the gathering crowd and tried to sense their common mood.

They parted to let him through, one man calling, 'You're wasting your food in there, Rube.' Someone else laughed. Overman walked on, not replying.

When he and Potsy were clear, he said, 'There's still some joking back there. They aren't worked up enough yet.'

'It won't be long,' Potsy said in his sad voice. 'Monk keeps stirring them up. It'll just take one match to light the torch.'

'Then we'll try to make sure it's our match,' Overman said.

He gave sharp orders to Potsy and then went to the hotel. He found Helene Colson in her front office. She beckoned him in and he saw that the work she was doing was all pretense.

Overman said, 'That mob won't wait much longer, Helene. Ross is a stubborn man. He wants no help. Especially from you.'

'Not from me—especially?' she queried bleakly.

'A man doesn't like to see his woman involved in something like this.'

Helene had never felt a closeness to Rube Overman, knowing that his dislike of her father had long ago extended itself to her. But now their mutual concern for Ross drew them together. 'His woman? From what I hear, she's already involved herself.'

Rube felt satisfaction. 'There's also talk that Eden Bruce and your bookkeeper Walsh have been working together.' He looked at her. 'And considering their past together . . .'

'So you know that, too,' Helene murmured. She thought, If Chet is using her against me and against Ross . . . She did not understand what Walsh would gain by such maneuvering, what he could do without her.

'What can I do?' she demanded suddenly.

Overman said, 'There are a pair of guards planted in the alley by Ross's cell. You can get rid of them and talk to Ross. If you can learn where Walsh and the girl might be, you can take these men I hear you've hired and ride.'

'I'll break Ross out and take him with me,' she said.

'He wants no help,' Overman repeated. 'But you can leave the way clear for him to help himself.'

'What good is my riding then?'

He said softly, 'To bring back Walsh and Eden Bruce to face Monk Ryker down with. To give the mob something to turn on besides Ross Millard.'

It could be done, she thought. The half-dozen men she had bought would do as she said, and Chet Walsh and the few he might have could hardly stand against them.

The irony of it flooded over her. If she brought Chet Walsh back, where was she? Where were her plans?

There was only one answer—to find out from Walsh himself where he stood, and then make her decision. She rose. 'All right, Rube. I'll do it your way.'

Overman went out, keeping his slow, steady pace until he was in his office at the Big Hat. Then he called Potsy in and gave him succinct orders.

Potsy said, when Overman was through, 'The Mexican is back. He moves like a shadow, that boy.'

'Send him in.' It had taken a great deal of effort the night before to get over to Blas Lamesa that he wanted him to trail Chet Walsh and Eden Bruce, to keep away from them unless Eden's life was threatened. And to return only after dark to report.

Blas Lamesa came in now, his dark face drawn from fatigue, limping slightly. He sat down at Overman's gesture and gratefully drank the glass of wine Overman poured for him. He drew a sheet of paper toward him, took a pencil and made a rough but serviceable sketch of the hill country. Overman's eyes followed the thick line that appeared, shaping into the wagon road. He saw the mark that was the tiny cabin high in the mountains, saw the X that blotted it out.

Blas Lamesa searched his memory and said, 'Burn. She burn.'

Overman nodded. Slowly the picture took form. He had to do some guessing but he was certain he had it straight. Sweeney was dead, shot by Chet Walsh. Eden Bruce, in attempting to save Cap Mills, had been taken with Cap by Walsh and Pickett. All of them were now in the box canyon behind the logging camp.

Blas Lamesa said, 'Ross?'

'Jail.' The Mexican's face was blank. Overman tried again. 'Hoosegow—' The word came to him. *'Carcel.'*

Lamesa got to his feet and started for the door. Overman stopped him. Carefully, patiently, he explained what they must do. Blas Lamesa listened, nodding when he understood. Overman supplemented his talk with a sketch and finally the boy nodded and sat down to wait.

Overman called Potsy in. 'Get this message to Helene Colson and to the sheriff,' he said. 'Walsh is holed up in the box canyon behind the logging camp up near the Hump. When she rides out, we'll be ready.'

Potsy slipped off and Overman looked at Blas Lamesa. 'It won't be long now—if it works.'

\*　　　\*　　　\*

Ross turned to see his father standing at the bars. 'How's it going?' He tried to sound casual.

The sheriff grunted. 'That scrawny Pickett rode in to town. He's telling it around that you hired him and Sweeney to work over Cap Mills' land and that you shot Sweeney last night to keep him quiet, and he got away by sheer luck.'

'Is that your belief?'

'If it is,' the sheriff said heavily, 'then I raised a poor son, didn't I?' He added, 'I got a message that Walsh is holed up behind the logging camp.'

'So I thought,' Ross said. He walked up to the barred door. 'How much time do I have?'

'No more than enough,' his father said dryly, and stopped with his back turned.

Ross's arm snaked out and lifted his father's gun from its holster. 'Sorry,' he said, 'but—'

The sheriff turned, his face blank. 'If you think you can get anywhere this way—'

'Just open the door,' Ross said.

'I'll have to form a posse and go after you,' Millard warned him.

'I expect that. Give me a half hour. It'll be enough—'

Matt Millard unlocked the cell door. Ross walked down the corridor and into the office. Keeping low and out of sight of the windows, he went to his father's arsenal. He selected a hand gun and a carbine, leaving the sheriff's weapon on the desk. Then he went to the side door.

He turned and saw his father standing in the corridor door, his face drawn and old and he knew what it had cost him to break every precedent he had lived by for so long. Ross thought, He must believe in me some, then, and the feeling was warming.

He said, 'Thanks,' and reached for the door latch.

His hand fell away as the sudden roar of guns burst outside. Someone cried, 'Jailbreak. They're breaking him out!'

The sheriff crossed to the desk and blew out the lamp. Ross jerked the door open and slipped into the night.

The side door opened onto a narrow alley between the jailhouse and the restaurant. He stopped at the corner, listening to the feet of running men as they discovered the guards unconscious beneath the cell window.

That way was blocked and he swung about as he heard the soft steps of a horse coming from the street toward him. He waited, the carbine lifted. Then he saw, by the faint light of the clouded moon, the slender form of Blas Lamesa.

'*Amigo*,' Lamesa said huskily, and slipped out of the saddle. 'Saloon,' he said. He repeated it, pointing.

Ross climbed aboard the horse and headed

for the street. He paused at the corner of the building. Men boiled here, too, but the mob was scattered, some seeking shelter, others on their horses.

Ross raked his heels into the horse's flanks. It gathered speed, and shot across the dark street.

A man cried, 'There goes one!' and a gun slammed at him.

He drove the horse between two buildings, into a lane of darkness, toward the alley that ran behind the Big Hat.

'It's Millard!' someone yelled, and bullets searched the darkness at his back. At the mouth of the alley, Ross left the horse, slapping it on the rump, sending it straight across the field there, and then crouched in shadow, waiting.

The riders plunged on, following the fleeing animal, and Ross turned and ran down the alley to the rear of the saloon. He slipped inside the door to find the place dark. A voice said, 'Ross?' It was Potsy.

'Is this Rube's idea?' Ross demanded.

'Rube's idea,' Potsy agreed. 'He wasn't ready, but this Pickett hit town and started spreading his story and—'

'So I know,' Ross interrupted. 'Tell Rube I'm obliged, anyway.' He turned and went back into the alley, still clutching the carbine.

The noise from the street was lessening. He could hear his father's strident voice when he neared the street.

'I want men for a posse. I know where he'll go, I tell you.'

And closer to Ross, the deep, caustic voice of Monk Ryker: 'And lead you on a wild-goose chase. Ride with me and . . .'

Ross moved along the side of the saloon and stood where he could see into the street. They were gathering, some about the jail where Matt Millard stood, others coming toward Monk Ryker, who stood by the hotel. Ross made out Pickett beside Monk. He saw Monk speak to the little man and watched as Pickett turned and ducked into the darkness of the hotel lobby.

The entire town was without lights, Ross saw. No man wanted to risk his home or his business by making a target for some wild one to shoot at. Now he turned and went to the alley and down it to the bottom of the town. Near where Cap Mills had been shot at that night, he slipped across the street, and came up to the hotel at the rear.

He went in through the kitchen, moving carefully. He heard the soft scuffle of footsteps coming from above and he turned, seeking the back stairs.

He came onto Pickett in Chet Walsh's room, and stood in the doorway, watching the man in the dim light working over the drawers of the bureau.

Ross said, 'Looking for something?'

Pickett turned, a shout of fear dying in his throat. 'Millard!'

Ross said, 'There isn't much time, Pickett. I'm going to tie you up and leave you here—if you tell it straight. If you don't—one more gunshot will make no difference.' He moved the carbine forward. 'I'm listening.'

'I don't know nothing,' Pickett whined.

Ross levered the carbine. 'Five seconds. No more.'

It was almost as though a clock ticked in the room. Ross said, 'That's one.' Then, softly, 'Two.'

The man was crumbling.

'Three.'

'I'll tell you what I know,' Pickett babbled at him.

'I'm listening.'

'I was looking for Walsh's papers,' Pickett said hurriedly. 'Monk told me he had some diagrams I was to get.' Ross listened to the story from the beginning, when Pickett was hired, to the moves by Monk to use him against Walsh to gain a bigger share, and finally, to the fact that Chet Walsh held both Cap Mills and Eden Bruce prisoner.

'Ah,' Ross said. Eden was Walsh's prisoner, not his helper. 'Go on.'

There was little more. Ross heard the man out and then stepped forward and drove the gun butt against the side of his head. Pickett sprawled awkwardly on the thin rug of the floor.

Ross turned his attention to the bureau, risking a match flame held low in the drawers. He found what he sought in the bottom one beneath a pile of fancy shirts. He got the lamp and carried it to the wardrobe against the wall, where he lighted it. By the dim light he examined the papers.

Slowly they formed the picture. Here was the dry basin land cut into parcels, ditched for irrigation. Here was a dam on Cap Mills' creek, and finally there was a bill of sale signed over by Ross Millard to Helene Colson for the sum of fifteen thousand dollars.

Ross folded the papers and thrust them inside his shirt, blew out the lamp, and walked from the hotel room. The town stood dark and empty of life except for the Big Hat, which was once more throwing its yellow lamplight across the board sidewalk and into the street. Ross went in the rear door.

The big room was empty and Ross walked on up the stairs and knocked at the office door. Rube Overman's deep, gentle voice told him to come in. He opened the door and saw Overman at his desk. The man looked weary.

'Its about time. I've got three men hunting you. There's a horse waiting. And there's not much time.'

Ross reached into his shirt and took out the papers. 'I found these in Walsh's room.'

The saloon owner read them slowly and

then pushed them aside. 'So Helene is in with Walsh,' he said in a half whisper. 'I should have known. I half suspected, but I took the chance.'

'Let her men and the posse and Monk's crew cut each other down,' Ross said. 'Let them find Cap and we'll see how Walsh gets out of this.' He grinned viciously. 'I'll sit this one out.'

'You fool,' Rube cried. 'Helene rode with those men of hers.'

'Helene can ride to hell for all of me,' Ross said flatly.

'And she rode to get Eden. Don't you see . . .' Quickly, Overman told him the maneuver he had made to get Helene to take her men against Walsh. 'But if she's in with him, she'll protect him.'

Ross said with intense quietness, 'And to do that they'll have to get rid of Cap and Eden.'

'Helene hates Eden. She hates her for what she means to you—or at least what she thinks she means to you. And she also hates Eden for what she's meant and could mean again to Walsh. What chance will Eden have against Helene?'

The sudden urgency of this welled up in Ross and his mind straightened out, seeing how Helene had maneuvered him, how he had played into her hands that night.

'That horse, Rube?'

'Out back, waiting—with Blas.'

Ross turned and ran, the carbine bumping against his leg. He found the horse and the Mexican. They climbed into their saddles and headed out of town.

Ross rode a big, solid bay, long-legged, a ground-eater. He forced it to the limit. He calculated the start the others had on him, and knew that it was too great.

Halfway along the wagon road, he swung to his left, cutting through the forest and riding almost parallel to the meadow. Blas Lamesa followed. Ross angled northward until a rounded edge of hill halted him abruptly.

He left his horse in a small clearing and squatted on the ground, smoothing a space in the dirt. Blas Lamesa joined him, and Ross struck a match. With a twig he roughly sketched where they were in relation to the meadow. Blas nodded as the twig made a dotted line uphill and then abruptly dropped down to the bottom of the box canyon.

'It's a mean climb,' Ross said. 'And if we slip—a straight drop down.' Blas Lamesa only nodded.

They rode their horses as far up the slope as the terrain would permit and then, leaving them, Ross led the way. Soon they were out of the timber and onto bare rock. Ross climbed steadily, aware only when he rested of the stiffness of his wound and the pain in his arm. Blas followed silently.

They swung around a ridge of rock and

halted, lying belly-down at the edge of a steep pitch. Above them, the moon fought to break through scudding clouds, driven on a wind that keened around them, icy at this altitude. Suddenly the clouds split and the moon came hard and bright through the rift, lighting the landscape below.

The meadow lay within their view. Monk was swinging his men in a slow, wide arc, planning to block off the posse making for the mouth of the canyon. There was no sign of Helene and her crew.

The flame of guns shone like match flares in the night below. A shift in the wind brought the sounds of the guns up to the ledge where Ross and Blas lay.

Ross thought, Helene? And then he understood. She had gone in to join Walsh. And with Monk leading his crew, obviously on the same side, the posse would have little chance. For Cap and Eden, there could be only one answer.

## CHAPTER SIXTEEN

Helene rode at the head of her crew, forcing her flagging horse. She was far from an expert horsewoman and only by sheer determination did she manage to stay in the saddle.

She led the way openly across the meadow

to the log building. There, she slipped to the ground, rested a moment, and then walked slowly to the far corner. She cupped her hands about her mouth.

'Chet!'

The echo of her voice came back from the hills, faint and slow. She called again and waited. From the screen of timber ahead, a voice answered:

'Helene?'

She said quietly, 'I came with that crew you hired for me, Chet. Come out with your hands up. We have some talking to do.'

Walsh's voice was filled with amusement. 'All right, boys, bring her in.'

The six closed about her and the leader, a burly man, said, 'Sorry, ma'am. But he's the boss.'

'I hired you,' she cried. 'It's my money that pays you.'

'Maybe. But his promises to get fatter faster.'

In silence, they went through the screen of brush to the little cabin. Walsh stood in the open doorway, gun in hand. He said, 'Spread out and keep watch. This isn't over.'

'Over,' the leader grunted. 'There's hell blowing in that town. And it'll bust up here, if I know that sheriff.'

Walsh stepped inside, motioning Helene to precede him. She looked around, and her eyes rested on Cap Mills and Eden Bruce at the far end of the room. They sat in such a position that she could not see the leg chains holding each.

'Well?' she demanded. 'Talk fast, Chet.'

He offered her his best smile. 'I tried to get a message to you—through Pickett. Obviously it didn't come, or you wouldn't have this attitude.'

'I got no message.' She walked to a chair near the fire and sat down heavily, shaking a little from the ride.

'I told Pickett to tell you to get Millard and bring him here,' he said. 'One of the boys you rode with was up earlier today with a report that Millard was in jail and about to be lynched.'

'And you were going to save him.' She looked scornfully at him. 'That story will work no longer, Chet. I know where you stand—you and her.' She nodded toward Eden Bruce.

Walsh laughed. 'I'm not accustomed to chaining my women. And she's very much chained.' He added dryly, 'She followed me last night, hoping I'd lead her to Millard. I did—but not in the way she wanted.'

Eden showed a sign of life for the first time. 'Is Ross all right?' she demanded.

Helene glanced at her. 'When I left, he was,' she said. She turned back to Walsh. 'That explains nothing, Chet.'

He could sense a lessening of her anger. He said, 'Due to Millard's meddling and Monk's

169

idea to get more money, things have been forcibly changed, my dear.'

'Meaning?'

'Meaning that you'll have to make a choice.' He spread his hands. 'We'll have to choose between Millard and the success of the scheme.'

Helene said slowly, 'Between Ross and the—'

He put it quietly, interrupting her. 'And the millions there are for the taking.'

'We can do nothing without the land,' she said. She knew now that as far as Cap Mills and the girl were concerned, they did not count. She had steeled herself to accept the old man's sacrifice. Eden Bruce, she felt, looking at her in man's clothing, her face stained and scratched, her hair awry—Eden Bruce, she herself could have killed with no compunction.

'I have a bill of sale that will pass muster anywhere,' he confessed. 'It's made out to you, signed by Ross Millard. That part is taken care of.'

A man threw open the door. 'They're coming, two damned hordes of them. Ryker's is the leading one and gaining ground.'

'Go set your men up,' Walsh commanded. 'We can hold this place as long as we need to.' He looked back at Helene. 'Someone has to be the goat for this, my dear. Millard is the only logical one.' His eyes measured her.

Helene rose and walked to the stove and stood before it. She glanced toward the rear of the room and the look she received from Cap Mills made her crawl inside. Then her eyes rested on Eden Bruce, and she saw nothing but defiance and contempt for her. She cried, 'You're Ross's woman, aren't you?'

'Any time he'll have me, yes,' Eden answered quietly.

'And he will, by God,' Cap Mills said. 'She's the kind a man can ride with—any time, anyplace.'

Helene turned her back on them. 'All right, Chet. Where do we go from here?'

'Just watch me,' he said. He walked to her and put his hands on her shoulders and looked down into her face. With the slow smile shaping his lips, he put them against her mouth. She neither resisted nor responded. She simply stood with her arms hanging.

He stepped back. 'Soon it will be different. You're tired now, Helene.'

She put her hand to her mouth where his lips had rested. She thought, Who else but this kind of man would have me now? She said, 'Soon it will be different, Chet. When I'm rested.'

He walked out, leaving her. She ignored the silent pair at the end of the room, seating herself before the fire.

Walsh moved through the dark, calling softly to his men. He said, 'I want to talk to

Monk.'

'Monk wants to talk to you,' a voice rumbled from his side. Walsh jumped about and then stood motionless. Monk was standing with his back to a tree, not five feet away. His gun was pointed at Walsh's belly. He said, 'I sent Pickett to your room for some plans, Walsh. By now, my side will have all the information. I don't think I need you or Mills or Millard any more.'

'That's where you're wrong,' Walsh said coolly. 'It's a big scheme, Monk, the kind that takes big money to start it. Have you a hundred thousand to build a dam and advertise for farmers and pay their rail and stage fares here? Have you more to loan them while they get started, to carry them for a couple of years until their crops come in, to stake them to cattle and barns and houses?'

'No,' Monk said easily, 'but Helene Colson will go for that kind of proposition.'

'So she will,' Walsh told him, amusement in his voice. 'So she has. Come on in the cabin and meet her.' His voice lashed out. 'Who do you think paid for all this to begin with?'

'I should have known,' Monk said. 'So that's the way it is. All right, let's go in and talk to her.' He was laughing, too. 'Maybe we can make a deal. I have a good crew out there, Walsh, and the sheriff is riding against you with half the town behind him.'

Walsh started for the cabin and Monk

followed, favoring his wounded leg. Helene glanced up and then stood. Monk shut the door and put his back to it.

'Howdy, Miss Colson. Walsh here tells me you and him have it all set up. Only it happens one of my men got the plans.'

'More can be drawn,' Walsh said. 'That means nothing.'

Monk shrugged. 'So they can. Only I have the men and I have the power. And I got enough evidence to tell around the town to make things uncomfortable.'

'What do you want?'

'A third,' Monk said. 'No more. Just my third.'

Walsh laughed at him. Monk shrugged again. 'Millard broke out of jail, Walsh. And the sheriff helped him, so I figure. That means the law believes his story. And that means more'n one person knows your part in it. The town would never deal with you, Walsh, once the truth came out.'

'Nor you,' Walsh said.

'Me,' Monk said. 'I fought Ross all my life. Anything I do to him is part of that fight. They don't know my part in this. Only you and the lady and Pickett. Pickett won't talk. The lady won't talk—because she can't swing this alone.' He smiled at Walsh. 'And you won't talk because you're going to be like Millard.' His gun came up swiftly. 'Dead, Walsh.'

Walsh saw it in Monk's eyes before his gun

hand moved. He threw himself to one side, his hand going for his own gun. Helene Colson stood motionless. Chet Walsh was a devious man, unable to play the game he had made up in a straight line. She understood how she must do this.

Monk's gun hammered loudly, kicking dirt from the floor by Walsh's feet. Chet Walsh stopped moving, his gun swinging around. Monk tried to line up another shot. His leg gave way and he fell heavily, his gun beneath him as he rolled frantically, trying to get into position.

Helene said coolly, 'Chet!'

Walsh's head came around and he saw the gun in her hand. At that instant, Monk freed his arm and fired. The bullet caught Walsh high in the chest and drove him back against the wall. His gun fell from his fingers. He slid down the wall and fell across the gun and lay still.

There was a pounding of feet and the door burst open. The leader of the hired crew stood there. Helene glanced at him and gestured with the gun. 'This is boss now,' she said. 'And the money that pays you is mine.'

His eyes took in the situation, then he nodded. 'What you say goes with us, ma'am.'

Cap Mills said, 'I'll double what she pays.'

Monk turned, his gun lifted. Helene stepped forward. 'Not yet,' she cried at him. 'Chet had a bill of sale for the place. Until we get that, we might need Cap.'

Monk's arm dropped. The man in the doorway said, 'The posse is halfway across the meadow, fellow.'

Monk turned. 'We'll block 'em for a while, fan out and then fade into the trees. When they come in the open around the corner of the log camp, you can shoot 'em like sitting ducks. Get that sheriff first.' He limped for the door. 'And watch for Millard.'

Cap Mills called, 'Remember my offer, you.'

Helene sat still, not looking at Cap Mills, not looking at the body lying so close on the floor. She heard the first shots, scattered, and then rising to a crescendo. She thought, But what if they break through?

And now she looked at the pair chained at the end of the room and back at Chet Walsh, and it shaped up in her mind what she must do. If Eden Bruce lay dead by Walsh and she sat where the girl was, chained, then who was to say what had happened but herself? It would mean sacrificing Cap Mills sooner than she liked, but it was the chance she would have to take.

She went to Walsh and found the key to the leg chains and then she returned to her chair, holding her gun and looking toward Eden Bruce. If they broke through . . .

# CHAPTER SEVENTEEN

Ross paused with the last steep drop to the box canyon at his feet. Beside him, Blas Lamesa clung to a sharp shard of rock. The roll of guns from the meadow was steady now. From his position, Ross could see the way the lines were formed, and he understood the strategy. The posse would drive for the screen and Monk would pull his men and the crew that the posse was not aware of and cut them down as they rode by.

'Let's go,' he said abruptly. He started down a narrow cut, pushing at the sides with his hands and knees to brace himself, edging downward. Once he slipped and had to thrust his knees violently against rock to hold himself. He felt the skin rip back and the blood start and felt the bullet-burn in his belly and he wondered how much longer he could hold out.

Below, the noise of the guns was lessening. They'd be pulling back now, he thought. And then he came around a ledge and saw the one yellow light from the cabin. There was enough glow for him to see what lay below: Ten feet of rock, sheer-faced, without a hold. He called in a low voice to Blas, 'Have to jump it,' kicked back with his feet and pushed with his hands. His feet struck the heavy grass of the canyon floor, sank in rank muck; and then he was pitched forward. He rolled, came to his feet and moved aside. Blas Lamesa landed beside him fighting for the breath that had been jarred from his body.

Ross broke into a run for the cabin. He paused in the shadow of the corner and then eased up until he could peer in the window. What he saw was plain enough. Cap and Eden Bruce at one end of the room, Helene Colson, with a gun, at the other. He drew Blas Lamesa to him and let him have a look. Then they eased down.

Ross spoke carefully, and prayed that the Mexican boy understood him. Then he slipped to the door. He saw Blas posed by the window, gun butt lifted. With a nod, he reached out and threw the door open.

Helene turned as he leaped in. The window glass shattered and Blas Lamesa's face appeared, his gun held steadily over the sill.

'Ross! Thank God!'

'Watch her!' Cap Mills shouted. 'Watch her, boy! She's a witch, that one. Ask Walsh there.'

Ross saw Walsh's body. He looked at Helene. 'Come on, Cap,' he said. 'You and Eden. Blas has things covered.'

'We're chained, Ross,' Eden Bruce said quietly. 'She has the key.'

Helene said desperately, 'Ross, I was only—'

His hand licked out and caught her gun, ripping it from her hand. 'I saw the bill of sale

177

and the plans, Helene. Give me that key.'

She looked at his face and then darted backward, against the wall. She lifted her hand and dropped the key into the bosom of her shirt.

'There isn't much time, Ross. There are too many against you—and if I called, they'd come fast enough.'

'So they might.' He walked toward her, unyielding. 'But Blas will shoot if you do call, Helene.' He lifted his hand, and slowly brought it down. His fingers caught the top of her shirt and underclothing and ripped.

The key fell to the floor, and Ross bent and picked it up. He walked to Cap Mills and handed him the key and Helene's gun. 'As she said, Cap. There's little time.'

Outside, the night was split with the boom of hand guns. Ross ran for the door, beckoning to Blas Lamesa. He untied one of the horses at the hitch rail and pulled himself into the saddle. Blas followed suit and they swung toward the screen of timber.

'Now!' Ross cried. His carbine raked the timber, cutting a swath through branches and brush. A man cried out in alarm, another in pain.

'Out of there!' Ross shouted. 'With your hands up.'

A bullet slapped by his head and he fired at the burst of flame from the gun. The man screamed and came forward, stumbled and

178

pitched on his face. Off to Ross's right, Blas Lamesa fired, and from the left came the sound of a gun and then another. Ross turned and saw Cap Mills and Eden Bruce, using their guns.

Others came out, four of them with their hands up. Ross said, 'Into the cabin, all of you. Cap—'

'I know what to do, boy. Eden, give me a hand with these gents.'

Ross rode as near the screen as he dared. He called:

'Sheriff! Dad! Watch your flanks. Watch for Monk Ryker on your flanks.'

A gun went off, sending bits of pine needle down on him. Someone swore. A voice queried, 'Ross?'

'Watch your flanks . . .'

The screen broke as men pounded through it. Guns spoke from the timber. On foot now, Ross slipped through the trees the way Monk had come into the canyon, seeing the flashes of men shooting into the flanks of the posse as the men of that group sought refuge in the canyon.

He stopped short in the dark as he heard Monk's thick voice. 'Pinch in,' Monk was shouting. 'Don't let them get into the canyon or we've lost 'em. Get that sheriff, I told you. Pinch in!'

Ross could have reached out and touched Monk's horse. He stepped away from the protection of a tree. 'Monk, come out of that saddle.'

Monk saw Ross standing there, a shape in the dimness. His gun lifted and lowered again as he saw he had no chance.

'Call off your men,' Ross ordered.

'Go to hell.'

'You have a chance. Call off your men.'

'And the chance?'

'You're the gun fighter,' Ross said. 'We'll play it your way. Twenty paces and draw on the count.'

'And if I don't?'

'I'll shoot you out of that saddle,' Ross said.

Monk looked down and then away. 'Hold it,' he cried. 'Hold the fire. We're flanked. They boxed us!'

The shooting dribbled off. A man's voice raised questioningly. In answer came the shout of the sheriff from behind the screen. 'When they move, give it to them.'

'Ah,' Ross said to Monk. 'They're in.'

Monk came off his horse, favoring his bandaged leg. He tied the animal to a bush and started walking.

Ross said, 'That's far enough, Monk. Shoot on three.'

Monk stopped and began his turn. Ross waited, his gun in its holster, knowing that he was no man with a gun compared to Monk Ryker. But it was the bargain he had made.

Monk was halfway through his turn,

favoring his leg. It seemed to give out on him and he fell to one side. Ross caught the dull gleam of moonlight on the gun which Monk held as he fell, and he threw himself sideways. The bullet slammed into the tree where he had been standing. Monk was on his knees, a dark, poor target, searching for Ross.

Ross said, 'The advantage was all yours, Monk. Now it isn't.' Monk fired at the sound of his voice. Ross heard the bullet and then he fired at the flash, slowly and deliberately. He could hear the sound the lead made striking Monk's flesh, the noise choked up from Monk's throat. Then the silence of the forest clamped down. Ross holstered his gun and walked wearily toward the canyon.

\*　　　\*　　　\*

Cap Mills was standing in the doorway of the cabin with light streaming around him, looking at the men facing him, some empty-handed, others holding guns. 'You crazy parcel of idiots!' he shouted. 'Ross Millard kidnapping or killing a man in cold blood? By God, I ought to have Matt Millard arrest and horsewhip the lot of you.' He paused and took a deep breath. 'If it wasn't that he should be the most ashamed of all.'

Ross stepped into the light. 'Not the most,' he said quietly. 'The least.' He looked at his father. 'You ought to be more careful about letting prisoners get out of your jail, Sheriff.'

He walked past Cap. The old man winked at him. 'I'm giving 'em what they need, boy. Make 'em crawl.'

Ross said, 'I'm the one to do that.'

'Ah, no,' Cap Mills said. 'She's inside, waiting.'

He went in and Eden stood there. Blas Lamesa was not far from her, erect, a gun in his hands. He saw who it was and his teeth flashed whitely, then he stepped out of the door to stand by Cap Mills.

Ross walked up to Eden Bruce. 'Eden?' he said.

She came into his arms, fiercely, and he held her, feeling the strength of her body against his, knowing that what was past mattered not at all—that it was only what lay ahead that counted.

At last he took his lips from hers. 'When were you sure of me, my dear?' she asked.

'Not until I saw you chained so,' he admitted.

'As a wife,' she murmured, 'I'll have to walk the straight and narrow path.'

He said in a low tone, 'Eden, Helene—'

She put a hand to his lips. 'I know. While we—waited, she told me. With relish, hating me. She would have killed me in a few more moments.'

He pushed his hands over his face, as if trying to wipe away a bad dream. 'Where is she?'

'Gone,' Eden said. 'Cap led her off, and when Monk's men surrendered, she rode around them and back to town. She won't be there when we arrive, Ross.'

'No,' he admitted. He thought of Helene, knowing she had money enough and a country wide enough to hide in.

The development she and Walsh had planned would be carried out, but with a different end in view—one of benefit to everyone, not just Helene. Whether she would ever know did not occur to Ross. He would not see her again. It was like a weight slipping from his shoulders. He lifted his arms and drew Eden to him again.

\*　　　\*　　　\*

Cap Mills glowered down from the stagecoach at the crowd gathered to see him off. 'You,' he said to Ross and Eden, 'you see that I get my half of the profits now. I'm going to live high and wide on the coast.' He glowered at the remainder of the crowd. 'I want every one of you to notice something. I'm going to Portland. I'm riding this stage and I ain't dead or kidnapped. Remember that, the whole cloth-headed pack of you!'

He disappeared abruptly as the stage jerked into motion. Ross and Eden watched it out of sight, and then walked away arm in arm.

We hope you have enjoyed this Large Print book. Other Chivers Press or Thorndike Press Large Print books are available at your library or directly from the publishers.

For more information about current and forthcoming titles, please call or write, without obligation, to:

Chivers Press Limited
Windsor Bridge Road
Bath BA2 3AX
England
Tel. (01225) 335336

OR

Thorndike Press
295 Kennedy Memorial Drive
Waterville
Maine 04901
USA

All our Large Print titles are designed for easy reading, and all our books are made to last.